A Heart to Come Home To

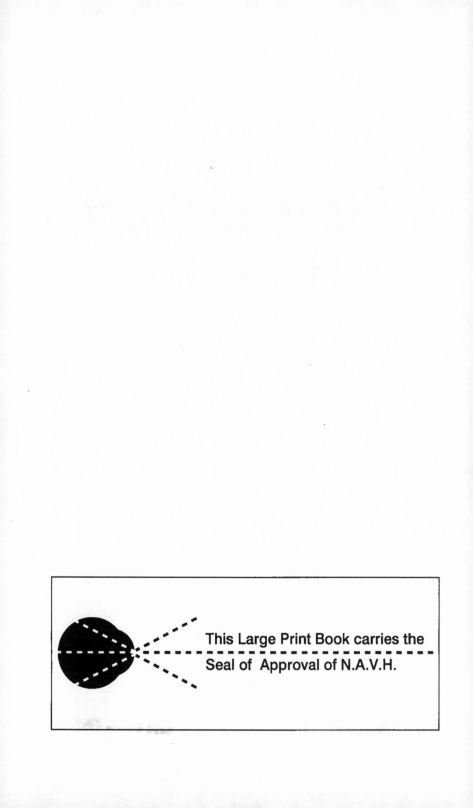

This Large Print Book carries the
Seal of Approval of N.A.V.H.

A Heart to Come Home To

Elizabeth Graham

Thorndike Press • Thorndike, Maine

Published in 2000 by arrangement with
Joyce Flaherty Literary Agency

Thorndike Large Print® Candlelight Series.

The tree indicium is a trademark of Thorndike Press.

The text of this Large Print edition is unabridged.
Other aspects of the book may vary from the original edition.

Set in 16 pt. Plantin by Al Chase.

Printed in the United States on permanent paper.

Library of Congress Cataloging-in-Publication Data
Graham, Elizabeth, 1939–
    A heart to come home to / Elizabeth Graham.
      p.   cm.
    ISBN 0-7862-2267-0 (lg. print : hc : alk. paper)
    1. Inheritance and succession — Fiction. 2. Home
ownership — Fiction. 3. Large type books. I. Title.
PS3566.A7565 H43 2000
  813′.54—dc21   99-047168

For my children:
Laura; Lewis, Jr.; Robert; and Susan.

And for my grandchildren:
Jennifer, Amy, and Matthew.

Chapter One

Who was that man and why was he staring at me so coldly? I knew that I'd never seen him before in my life. I shifted my weight and returned my attention to the minister, who was saying one last prayer for Great-Aunt Edith at her graveside. Tears filled my eyes and trickled down my cheeks. I wiped them away, wishing for the dozenth time since getting the telephone call three days ago that I'd somehow managed to visit her while she was alive.

I hadn't been back to Cedar Grove since my parents had moved us to Los Angeles twelve years ago, when I was fourteen. They were both killed in a car crash four years later, leaving me on my own. Aunt Edith offered me a home then, but I was ready to start college and the thought of leaving the excitement of L.A. for a little town in central Pennsylvania had no appeal.

When the service was over, I glanced up and saw the dark-haired man staring at me again as if he knew me and didn't like me. It made me feel uncomfortable. I turned away and said good-bye to Blythe Cole, my aunt's next-door neighbor and longtime friend. I walked back to my rented car with Mr. Preakness, Aunt Edith's lawyer.

"Then I'll see you in my office at ten tomorrow," he said.

I nodded. Mr. Preakness had been the one to call and tell me of Aunt Edith's death from a heart attack, and he'd also asked me to stay over for the reading of the will.

My rented motel room was lonely, and I decided to walk around Cedar Grove and see how much it had changed since we moved away all those years ago.

The town square was the same, I saw a few minutes later. It still had its park benches and meticulously maintained grass and flower beds. The pavilion where the school band used to play on Saturday nights was still there too. Nostalgia filled me as I sat down on a bench. I'd been in the band, and bitterly protested leaving.

The quiet peace of the town was so different from the noise and congestion of Los Angeles. It might be nice to live in a town like this again, I thought. And then I smiled at that idea.

I'd worked hard to get where I was. My parents had been loving, but they'd enjoyed a carefree lifestyle. Putting myself through college had been a struggle, but for three years now I'd been a second-grade teacher at a good school. I liked my work and had a nice apartment.

Of course, I had to fight freeway traffic for nearly an hour both night and morning, even though the school was only twenty miles from my apartment. And my rent had been raised again last month. And Bruce and I had split up a few weeks ago, after going together for more than two years.

I got up and walked back toward the motel, trying not to think about that. It didn't make me feel very good to find out that what I'd considered just a slow, cautious courtship on Bruce's part had in reality been nothing of the sort as far as he was concerned. I could still see his surprised face when I finally asked him what his intentions were.

"Why, we're just good friends, Dana, aren't we? Pals, you know. I don't plan to get serious about you or anyone else for a long time. I like my freedom too much."

Well, he certainly had his freedom, at least as far as I was concerned. I shrugged the memory away, but I knew it had left its mark. I wouldn't take anything for granted with a man ever again. And I wouldn't be in a hurry to get involved with another one, either.

I stopped at a small post office to buy some stamps. I'd brought a few bills with me that needed to be paid.

"Hi, there," a smiling, blond woman of about my own age greeted me. "Are you new in town? I don't remember seeing you before."

I smiled back, remembering how friendly everyone in Cedar Grove was. "I'm here for only a few days. I'm Edith Harris's great-niece."

"Dana? Are you Dana Gilbert?" she asked, her eyes widening a little. "Of course you are. You still have that beautiful red hair and those green eyes. I used to envy you, you know."

I made a face. "I always hated my hair and being called 'carrots' by all the boys. You look familiar to me too, but I can't remember your name."

Her smile widened. "I'm Lynn Hudson. We used to be in the same class before you moved to California."

Now I remembered. We hadn't really been friends, but we'd sat next to each other in a couple of classes, due to our last names beginning with G and H.

"I was sorry to hear about your aunt," she added.

Guilt hit me again. Why hadn't Aunt Edith let me know she had heart problems? I'd have tried to visit her, and maybe talk her into moving to California so that I could look after her. No, that was a crazy idea. She would never have left Cedar Grove.

"I'm sorry too," I told Lynn. "I wish I could have seen her again."

"So I guess you'll be heading back to the big city in a couple of days?"

I thought I detected a note of envy in Lynn's voice. "Yes," I said.

"After L.A., this must seem like a sleepy little burg to you."

Now I *knew* there was envy in her voice. "Actually, I was just thinking how nice and peaceful it is."

Lynn laughed. "You don't have to be polite. I'd love to get out of here, see the country a little."

"I'm not trying to be polite. I really do like it here."

Later, at bedtime, as I tried to read myself to sleep in my motel room, I thought about my chat with Lynn. I did like the town. As much as Lynn wanted to get away from it, I found myself wishing that somehow I could stay.

"There's no money, I'm afraid," Mr. Preakness told me the next morning. "But your aunt left you all she had — her house and the ten acres of land."

11

I stared at him. I shouldn't have been surprised, because as far as I knew, Aunt Edith had no other relatives but me. I was, though. Somehow, I'd never expected this. I bit my lip, then looked back at the man who'd been Aunt Edith's lawyer for forty years.

"But I live in California," I finally told him. "I don't know what to do with the house."

He nodded. "It's an old house, but soundly built," he said. "And, of course, land is getting more valuable all the time. You might consider selling it."

Guilt struck again. Sell Aunt Edith's house? How could I do such a thing? She shouldn't even have left it to me. She didn't owe me anything. I got up and gave him my hand. "I'll have to think about it."

His hand was wrinkled but his grip was still firm. "Of course," he said.

A few minutes later I opened the rusty front gate and walked into the yard. Its white paint was dingy and peeling, and a dark-green shutter hung from one hinge, but, just as Mr. Preakness had said, the house looked solid and well built. An old, overgrown lilac bush that I remembered playing in as a child still grew in a corner of the yard, along with some straggly rosebushes here and there.

I walked up the cobblestone walk and onto Aunt Edith's porch. No, I corrected myself, it was my porch now. I still felt very uncomfortable to know that.

I inserted the key Mr. Preakness had given me into the tarnished brass plate and turned it. With a protesting screech, the heavy oak door opened and I pushed it wider. A dry, musty smell hit me as I walked into the front hallway. It wasn't unpleasant, though. Aunt Edith's house had always smelled like this, I remembered amid a surge of nostalgia.

The faded wallpaper was the same as it had always been, and memories rushed in fast and thick now as I walked through the downstairs rooms. *Everything* was just the same. Aunt Edith hadn't changed a thing in all these years.

The old-fashioned kitchen had always been my favorite room. It still was. Morning sunshine streamed through the dusty windows, burnishing the cherry-wood cupboards and gilding a path across the oak table and the linoleum floor.

How many times had I sat at that table, eating Aunt Edith's gingerbread and drinking the tart, sweet lemonade that no one else could make as well?

The upstairs was just the same too — four bedrooms and the large bathroom that had been made from another bedroom years ago when the house was modernized. The large corner room that had been mine when I visited, with the window seats at the bow windows, still had the pink-sprigged spread and curtains, faded almost white now.

I walked to the window seat, lifted the lid, and then drew in my breath. The toys and treasures I'd collected were still there. I looked out the window, which faced on the back, where the meadowland stretched away, to end in the band of woods at the back of the property.

Beauty and peace settled down around me as I gazed out the window. How wonderful it would be to stay here, to live in this house. But I shook my head and turned away. *Don't be such an idiot, Dana Gilbert,* I scolded myself as I went back downstairs. *Your life is in L.A., not here in this old house in this little town. No way can you do anything about that.*

But even as I scolded myself, I knew I wasn't convinced. Maybe I *could* do something about it if I wanted to badly enough. . . .

Two weeks later I drove my five-year old

Toyota and a U-Haul trailer into the driveway of Aunt Edith's house. I'd burned my bridges for sure, and I still had butterflies in my stomach. I parked the car and got out and looked up at the old house. But I wasn't sorry I'd done it. And I could manage. I hadn't been completely stupid.

Before going back to L.A. I'd done some checking. I'd found out that there would be plenty of substitute-teacher work available at Cedar Grove Elementary when school started. Further, a first-grade teacher was leaving in December and they hadn't filled her job yet. I had a good chance at getting it.

By evening I'd unpacked the trailer and returned it to the local U-Haul dealer. I'd sold most of my furniture in L.A., keeping only my stereo and records, books and clothes, and a few personal possessions I couldn't bear to part with.

I took a long, hot shower and then put on Linda Ronstadt, noticing that the stereo looked modern and out of place in Aunt Edith's living room. Exhausted from the moving, I went to bed early in my old room upstairs.

Sometime in the night I woke out of a deep sleep because water was dripping on my face. I turned on the bedside light and saw a large, dark stain on the ceiling above the bed. While I watched, water splattered onto my face again. I wiped it away and realized that it was raining — hard.

Fumbling into a robe, I went up to the attic where I discovered not only the leak over my bed but several others, some dripping into pans and pails, some onto the attic floor.

Thoroughly awake and alarmed by now, I hurried to the kitchen and found a few more pans under the sink. I put them under the leaks, then tried to go back to sleep.

By six I gave up that idea and, after emptying the pots and pans, went downstairs and made a pot of strong coffee. Thank God, it had stopped raining, but I had to get the roof fixed — and soon. The kitchen faucet dripped badly too, I'd noticed yesterday, and so did the bathroom sink.

No doubt, as time went on, I would discover other things that needed attention. I didn't have to get out my bankbook to know that I had only enough savings to tide me over until school started and I could begin substitute teaching. But maybe, if I were very careful, I could squeeze out a little money for repairs.

No maybes about it, Dana, I told myself. *You have to find some money.* Poor Aunt

Edith. How long had the house been this neglected?

I wondered if Blythe Cole knew anyone who would work cheap. Then I remembered something. On my way here yesterday, I'd seen a man painting the outside of the Robinson house several houses down. Maybe he would be willing to do the repairs. No harm asking, I decided.

Two hours later, as I walked up the street, I was glad to see the jeans-clad man up on a ladder. He was painting the front of the house under the porch overhang. I'd been afraid, with all the rain, that he wouldn't be there today. He was well-built and muscular looking, I noticed.

Something about the shape of his dark head tugged at my memory. Did I know him? Was he, like Lynn, someone I'd gone to school with?

I walked closer, then said, "Excuse me. Could I talk with you?"

He swiped his brushful of spruce-green paint across the siding, then turned toward me, his dark eyebrows raised inquiringly.

I swallowed. I hadn't gone to school with him, but no wonder he'd looked a little familiar. He was the man who'd glared at me during the graveside service for Aunt Edith.

I now noticed a lot more about him than I

had then. His hair wasn't just dark — it was black. His eyes were a very dark brown, his firm chin had an interesting cleft, and he was tall and rugged. And I wished I was anywhere but here. But since I'd gone this far, I might as well talk to him. I managed a weak smile. "I'm Dana Gilbert and I just moved in down the road — the old Harris house?"

He gave me a cool, level look, and then nodded as if he knew the house. Which wasn't surprising. Since he'd been at Aunt Edith's services, he must have known her, and might even have been a friend of hers.

He wrapped his paintbrush in foil, placed it on top of the ladder, reached for a cloth wedged in between the rungs, and wiped his hands before descending the ladder. I noticed that his jeans and his sneakers weren't paint-spattered. I tried to imagine myself being that neat, and failed.

He was very good-looking, I saw as he reached the ground. A hunk, really. He must be in his early thirties, I decided. An unexpected flutter of awareness swept over me, making me even more uncomfortable.

"I'm Jordan Meade," he said. He hesitated a moment, then stuck out his hand. I hesitated even longer before extending my own. His large hand engulfed mine and felt warm and firm. His voice was deep and pleasant, even if it did sound cool and a little distant. I noticed that my heart was beating faster, and tried to ignore it.

I cleared my throat and removed my hand. "I didn't mean to take you from your job, but I saw you working here yesterday and wondered if you did handyman work and would have any free time when you finished painting this house. Aunt Ed— my house is in urgent need of some repairs."

His dark eyes stayed on mine for a long moment before he answered me. "What do you want done?" he finally asked.

I gave him a wry smile. "So far, all I've discovered are a badly leaking roof and some dripping faucets. But I'm sure that isn't everything that's wrong."

His firmly molded mouth didn't smile as he gazed back at me. "That house has a slate roof," he informed me, his words sounding somehow ominous.

He seemed very certain, so I shrugged. "If you say so. I don't know. Is that hard to repair?"

"About the worst. Replacement slate is not only hard to find but expensive. The roof is slick to work on, and fragile. It's easy to damage it while doing the repairs."

My heart sank. "Oh. I didn't know that. So I guess that means you wouldn't be interested in giving me an estimate on the job."

"I didn't say that." He indicated the house behind him. "This house has a slate roof too and I've repaired it. I know a place to buy the slate, and I've done the work on several houses."

Relief surged through me. Friendly he might not be, but that wasn't really necessary to get my roof fixed. "Then you'll come and give me an estimate?" I asked, trying to sound businesslike. "Of course, I know you have to finish this job first. I'm sure the Robinsons wouldn't appreciate my stealing you away."

As his eyes stared into mine again, something flickered in their depths. Now what had I said? Wasn't this how people handled such things in small towns? I'd been away too long to know.

Then, to my surprise, his mouth relaxed a little, almost into a smile. "Don't worry about that," he answered. "I'll be finished up here today, and I could look at your house tomorrow morning if you like. How about eight o'clock?"

"That would be great. Well, I'll let you get back to your painting. You do know the house, then?" *Maybe I should ask him if he'd been a friend of Aunt Edith's,* I thought. Then

I decided against it. Obviously, he wanted to keep this on a very businesslike footing.

He nodded. "I know the house."

There didn't seem to be anything more to say. I tried for a businesslike smile. "Well, I'll see you in the morning, then."

He nodded again, and I turned and walked back down the road, somehow sure that if I turned around, Jordan Meade would still be staring at my back.

I enjoyed the walk back, now that I had a promise of maybe getting some repairs done. It was a pleasant early-June morning, with a breeze that ruffled my shoulder-length hair. It was warm enough for shorts, and as soon as I got home, I'd get out of these jeans and put some on.

All the houses along this road, about a mile and a half out of Cedar Grove, had acreage. Aunt Edith's ten acres was the largest plot, I thought, remembering that hers was also the oldest house on the road and had once been part of a large farm. The road was even named after the family — Harris Road. There was some nice pastureland too.

A horse would be fun, I thought, and then at once dismissed that idea. I hadn't ridden a horse for years, and I couldn't afford one, anyway. Maybe someday. My living expenses would be a lot less here, especially since I didn't have rent or a house payment. I should be able to get along fine once I got a regular teaching job. *If* I got a regular teaching job, I reminded myself.

I finally realized I was deliberately concentrating on other things to keep from thinking about Jordan Meade. He'd made more of an impression on me than I liked, in spite of the obvious fact that he didn't like me much. That thought made me more than a little uncomfortable, mainly because I didn't understand why. We didn't even know each other, so how could he dislike me?

Then I realized something else: He didn't fit my mental picture of a handyman. He sounded too educated; he was too self-assured. *Oh, knock it off, Dana,* I told myself crossly. *Get your mind on something else.*

I would spend the afternoon giving the house a long overdue cleaning, I decided, and would forget about Jordan Meade until tomorrow morning. But first I would make a big pitcher of iced tea and have an early lunch.

An hour later, with lunch finished and the dishes washed, I headed upstairs with broom, mop, and other cleaning supplies. As I entered the front hallway, I thought I heard a scratching noise from outside. I stopped and listened. Yes, there it came again. Curious, I swung the heavy door open.

A small gray kitten looked up at me, mewing loudly. Then it darted between my legs and scuttled into the living room and under the old sofa, but exposing its little tail. I laughed out loud, it was so cute, and I walked quietly into the room, calling "Here, kitty, kitty." The kitten responded by moving farther under the couch.

I considered my options. I could reach under and try to pull it out. But that might hurt it and also give me some scratches. Luring it with food might work. I didn't have any cat food, but I did have tuna and milk.

I hurried to the kitchen and poured milk into a saucer. Then I opened a can of tuna and placed a spoonful on the saucer's edge. I carried it back to the living room and set it on the floor in front of the sofa, hoping that the kitten hadn't decided to hide somewhere else while I was gone.

I waited, crouching at the side, and in a few seconds the kitten cautiously poked out its small head and looked at the saucer of food. I slowly moved the saucer a little farther away and held my breath. Too hungry to be cautious now, the kitten darted out and over to the saucer, where it began to eat ravenously.

I didn't know how old it was, because I hadn't had a cat since we'd lived here in Cedar Grove years ago. But it was weaned, obviously, because it was having no trouble with the tuna and milk.

After a few minutes I decided that it had eaten enough for now, and I informed it, "Okay, baby, you can have more later." I scooped it up and held it against my T-shirt, caressing its back in an attempt to stop its hissing and spitting.

"Where did you come from?" I asked it when it had calmed down and settled against me. "I'd better see if you belong around here."

I glanced at my broom and mop, then shrugged. I could always clean house. Blythe Cole, who lived in the next house to the west of this one, might know its owner. Anyhow, I should stop in and let her know I'd moved in yesterday. She'd been so happy when she found out I wasn't going to sell the house but planned to live here.

And that had probably not been a wise decision, but I wasn't going to worry about it now. Holding the kitten firmly against my shirt, I walked across the wide side yard and then through the opening in the hedge between the two properties.

"I've never seen it before," Blythe told me. "Cute little thing, though." She smiled and pushed back her graying brown hair with a floury hand, her hazel eyes twinkling. "Come on in, Dana. I'm baking some sweet rolls."

I smiled at her, then shook my head. "Thanks, Blythe, but I can't. I need to find out who this squirt belongs to."

Blythe was a widow and she'd lived in her house since before we moved away from Cedar Grove. She was quite a bit younger than Aunt Edith and still very attractive.

"Well, I'm sure I have no idea," she said. "Someone may have just dumped the poor thing out. Why don't you keep it if you want to? There's always plenty of stray kittens around the countryside. Here, take some of these rolls with you."

A while later I went back into the house, still holding the kitten and with a litter pan and food in the car to bring in. I'd decided to keep him while I advertised in the local newspaper's lost-and-found section.

"I hope you're a genuine stray," I told him, running my hand gently down his back. He arched his spine, purring so loudly that his body shook. I set him down on the hall carpet where he promptly curled up in a patch of sunlight and went to sleep.

He was the color of smoke, I decided. "Smoke — that's a good name for you." *Uh-oh, Dana. You've named him and now he's yours for good.* Somehow, that thought didn't displease me at all. I would enjoy his company in this big old house.

Bringing in the cat supplies, I eyed the broom and mop still leaning against the stairway wall. I sighed. Better get to it. But first I would place the ad. I turned to the advertising section in the paper I'd picked up a few minutes ago and found the phone number. Then my eyes stopped on a column headed *Help Wanted.* For a small town, Cedar Grove wanted quite a lot of office help.

Maybe I could find some temporary office work to give me extra money for the house repairs. Was there a temp agency in town? I grabbed the phone book, glanced through its small yellow-page section, then put it back down, disappointed. I didn't want to get a permanent job, because school would be starting in a couple of months.

Then, my mind clicked on something. I'd put myself through college by typing at home for other students — term papers and so forth. I still had my electric typewriter, old but serviceable. And Cedar Grove had a popular liberal arts college that drew summer students from near and far. Bingo!

Five minutes later I felt a little better about my precarious financial position. I'd placed two ads — one for the kitten and another for my new enterprise, the Flying Fingers Secretarial Service.

There was a small study off the living room that would do fine as my home office. It already had a solid maple desk and a comfortable chair. All I had to do was set up my typewriter and lay in a supply of ribbons and paper.

"Back to downtown Cedar Grove," I told Smoke as I grabbed my purse and headed for the door. As cats will, he ignored me and continued with his nap.

Life in Cedar Grove was shaping up as quite busy, I thought as I headed down the road. Jordan Meade was nowhere to be seen around the Robinson house, which looked finished. I realized I was looking forward to seeing him in the morning, and not only because I needed my roof repaired.

And I'd put a stop to that line of thought right now, I told myself. I wasn't interested in getting to know any new men. After my experience with Bruce, caution was going to be my middle name from now on.

I grinned at my thoughts as I pulled onto the county blacktop. Jordan Meade would probably be extremely surprised to know that I was concerned about getting involved with him.

Chapter Two

Smoke started the night at the foot of my bed, and ended it curled up on my pillow, purring into my ear. "You can be glad I'm not allergic to cats," I told him when the alarm went off at six-thirty. I was glad too. His warm little body had been very comforting.

I washed my face, dressed, and headed downstairs for breakfast and my two cups of coffee before Jordan Meade arrived. I can't function before my morning coffee.

Smoke and I shared a companionable hour, and by the time a knock sounded on the front door promptly at eight, I was feeling up to tackling Jordan Meade. But I hoped that he wouldn't be as cool and distant as he'd been yesterday.

And if wishes were horses, beggars would ride too, as they say, I told myself as I swung the door open. His handsome face didn't look one speck friendlier than it had yesterday.

"Good morning," I said, stepping back to let him enter the house. "At least it isn't raining," I added cheerfully. I didn't know what he had against me, especially since he didn't even know me. But it wouldn't help matters any if I behaved the same way.

"Good morning," he answered, walking into the wide front hall. Something about the way he glanced around made me think that he was familiar with the house, and it reinforced my idea that he and Aunt Edith might have been friends.

"Do you want to check the roof first?" I asked. "But I'm not sure if there's a ladder." Why hadn't I *made* sure before I asked him to come?

"I have a ladder on my truck," Jordan answered, his glance coming to rest on my face. He gave me a leisurely once-over, starting at the top of my pulled-back hair and ending with my sneakered feet. "Yes, I'll check the roof."

I was beginning to feel annoyed at his manner, but I told myself to try to keep the cheerful act going. To that end, I asked him, "Would you like a cup of coffee first?" I wouldn't have dreamed of making such an offer to a workman in L.A., but Cedar Grove was different. However, I realized I probably should have checked him out with Blythe, who knew everyone in town.

He shook his head, as I'd been pretty sure he would. "No, I want to get started." He turned to the door again.

"Fine," I answered crisply, my store of

patience beginning to run out. He didn't have to be so darn rude about it. "I'll be in the kitchen when you're finished."

I heard scraping sounds overhead as I washed my few breakfast dishes. Smoke kept twining himself around my ankles in hope of more food. "You're an absolute pig," I told him, "and you don't need anything else. Go take a nap."

I heard a knock on the back door while I was wiping off the stove, and let Jordan Meade in. His blue T-shirt had smudges of dirt down the front, and so did his jeans. His wavy black hair was rumpled, but none of that made him any less attractive.

"It's pretty bad," he said without preliminary. "It needs quite a lot of slates replaced, and they're not in one or two locations, either, but all over the roof."

I could have told him that from the spacing of the pots and pans that were still up in the attic. I took a deep breath and looked him straight in the eye. "How much will it cost?"

He named a figure that sent my heart plunging to my ankles. No way could I afford that, not even if I had students lined up from here to the road with work for me to type, and that wasn't likely to happen.

I gave him a weak smile. "That's way

31

beyond my means. I guess I'll have to try to do the work myself."

A derisive smile seemed to be hovering around his mouth. "Do you have any idea how to do that kind of work?"

I shook my head, feeling my face reddening. "No, but I'm sure the library has some how-to books. I'm a quick learner."

"You'd better be *very* quick," he said, brushing at his sleeve. "It needs immediate repair before it rots out some of the structural supports."

"Thanks, I'll keep that in mind," I answered dryly, my heart sinking farther, into my shoes. "And thanks for your time. What do I owe you for the estimate?" No use in asking him to look at the dripping faucets or the water heater, which I'd discovered last night wasn't heating water much above lukewarm.

"No charge." For a moment, he looked at me in a slightly different way, as if he considered me not quite lower than plant life. Then he straightened up to his full height, which was considerable. "I'll be seeing you around, I guess, if you're going to be living here."

"I don't know if I'll be living here or not," I answered, realizing I was close to tears and horrified at the possibility of any of them escaping in his presence. "I may sell the place." I hated that thought, but what else could I do? My remarks about how-to books had been sheer bravado. I couldn't even drive a nail in straight for picture-hanging.

His glance hardened again. "Maybe that's a good idea. It's a nice old house and needs someone who can appreciate it." With that, he let himself out the back door.

Someone who could appreciate it? I felt like throwing something at his retreating back. What was the matter with the man? Did he hate the world, or was it only me?

As I listened to his truck starting up and leaving, I took deep breaths and tried to calm down. Finally, I got out my bike and rode for half an hour. I felt better when I returned home.

Should I go talk to Blythe? Maybe she could recommend someone who'd give me a better price. No, I decided in a minute. There was no use in that. Though Jordan Meade seemed to dislike me, I didn't think he'd taken advantage of my ignorance to quote me an outlandish price for repairs. And anyone else would have to come way down for me to be able to afford it.

There was only a single alternative if I wanted to stay in the house. As I'd said to Jordan, there were sure to be how-to books in the library. "Necessity is the mother of invention," I told Smoke, then headed out the door again, this time to the Toyota. Maybe I wasn't as klutzy with tools as I thought I was.

Early the next morning I carefully leaned the old ladder I'd found in the garage up against the side of the house. The ladder didn't look all that sturdy, but I hated to spend any of my very limited funds on a new one. Eyeing it skeptically, I put my foot on the first rung as I clutched the two slates I'd found in the attic and my hammer and box of nails.

It creaked and groaned, and I held my breath, half expecting my foot to go through a rung any second. I wondered how far you had to fall to do something really bad to yourself — like breaking a leg. I pictured myself, leg in a huge white cast, trying to figure out how to sit at my desk and type term papers for my as yet nonexistent clients.

Reaching the top rung at last, I let out my breath in relief and carefully eased myself up onto the sloping roof. I took a small step, and then, while my arms flailed wildly in the air, the slates, hammer, and nails all went sailing. Desperately, my heart pounding, I tried to keep my balance.

The hammer hit the ground with a thud, and those other noises were the slates breaking into a hundred or so pieces and the musical tinkle of dozens of scattering nails. I heard sliding sounds, and then a couple of pieces of slate moved past me and off the roof. In a moment, they, too, hit the ground.

Great. Just great. I'd not only dropped all my supplies and almost fallen, but I'd also damaged the roof even more. Somehow, I managed to get my trembling feet back on the ladder and down on the ground again. When Jordan Meade had said slates were slippery, he hadn't prepared me for the reality of the situation. No way could I attempt to fix that roof. I couldn't even stand up on it.

Gloomily, I shared lunch with Smoke, then stacked the how-to books on a corner of the big oak table. I'd never been the impulsive type, and deciding to leave my secure job in California and move here had been totally out of character. Was I going to have to go back there, tail between my legs, and try to get my old job back?

"No!" I said, pushing back my chair. I would go talk to Blythe, and maybe she could recommend someone to do just the barest minimum of repairs for right now. But Blythe wasn't home, I discovered a few minutes later. And her car was gone from the driveway too, which meant she wasn't just at a neighbor's or taking a walk.

Would Mr. Preakness know of anyone? Possibly, but I hated to bother him. Then I remembered Lynn Hudson, my former classmate in Cedar Grove's junior high school. She'd lived here all her life, just like Blythe.

The post office was deserted when I got there. Good. Lynn and I could talk. "Do you know any local handymen who work cheap?" I asked her without preliminary. "*Very* cheap?"

"Handymen?" Lynn repeated, frowning in thought while her curly blond hair sprang to life all around her animated face. Then she shrugged apologetically. "I'm afraid not, Dana. Dad's always done everything at home. I'm sorry."

I leaned on the window ledge separating us and sighed. "I know Cedar Grove isn't a big city, but surely Jordan Meade isn't the only person around who does painting and repairs."

There was such a long silence that I finally glanced up. Lynn was looking at me with an expression of pure astonishment on her pretty face. "Did you say *Jordan Meade?*" she asked.

"Yes. He was painting the Robinson house yesterday and I stopped by and asked him to give me an estimate, but no way can I afford his price." There was no point in telling her that Jordan Meade didn't seem to like me. I didn't think it had any bearing on my problem.

Lynn stared at me a moment longer. Then she grinned at me, her blue eyes dancing. "Honey, I hate to tell you this, but the Robinson place is now *owned* by Jordan Meade. And he's not a handyman." She shook her head as if at a hugely funny joke.

It was now my turn to stare as her information sank in. "Then why," I floundered, "didn't he tell me so? Why did he come to the house and give me an estimate for repairs?"

"I can't imagine, unless he was pulling your leg. He's a contractor — one of the best in the county. He also buys and restores old houses, and does a lot of the work himself. He's good at that too."

"He buys and restores old houses?" I repeated as I finally began to figure out what was going on. Or at least part of it. I still didn't know why Jordan Meade disliked me, but now I knew why his estimate had been so high.

Lynn nodded. "Yes, he's done real well at that, everyone says. He moved here about three years ago and has become one of the most successful businessmen in town. He's also on the town council and has a finger in all the pies."

I smiled at her grimly. "Thanks, Lynn, you've been very helpful." I turned and headed for the door, my destination firmly in mind.

"Wait!" she called after me. "Where are you going? What did I say?"

I waved at her. "I'll tell you later. Right now, I have something to discuss with a certain Mr. Jordan Meade."

Outside, I took a few deep breaths to try to calm down. It didn't help much. I got into the Toyota and drove back to Harris Road, my hands gripping the steering wheel so hard that they hurt.

Jordan Meade's red pickup truck was parked in the driveway of the house that I'd thought still belonged to the Robinson family. I hoped that meant he was somewhere around.

I parked alongside the pickup and walked to the house. It looked good, I had to admit. The fresh green paint made a nice contrast to the black shutters. Jordan Meade apparently knew what he was doing, as Lynn had said. I had no quarrel with that — just with his methods.

I punched the doorbell twice, then waited. My hand was poised to punch again when the door swung open. Jordan wore jeans and a T-shirt again, and he still was one of the handsomest men I'd ever seen. But I wasn't interested in that now.

I didn't bother to hide my feelings this time. "I'd like to talk to you," I said, my voice several degrees cooler than his had been with me.

His dark brows rose a little, but he stepped back and gestured for me to enter. "If it's about that estimate," he said, "I'm afraid I can't come down any."

The foyer we were standing in was familiar to me. I'd visited this house a few times with Aunt Edith when the Robinsons owned it. But it was also new and unfamiliar. As angry as I was, I couldn't help but notice how great it looked, how it had been remodeled without destroying its special qualities.

I took another deep breath and looked him straight in the eye. "It's about your estimate all right."

He looked back at me just as straight. "I

can't work any cheaper than that. My time is worth too much to me."

My lip curled. It really did; I could feel it. "Oh, I imagine it is," I said sweetly. "I'm sure it's worth a *great* deal more than that. I'll have to give you credit. You're a very smooth operator. You had me fooled."

His brows drew together in a frown. "I have no idea what you're talking about," he said flatly.

I raised my own eyebrows at that. "Let's stop playing games, Mr. Meade. I just talked to Lynn Hudson. She told me who you really are and what you do for a living."

I didn't know what I expected, but not the half smile that appeared on his face. "You make it sound like I'm a member of an organized crime family. I assure you, all my activities are legal."

Somehow, that made me even madder. "I didn't say they weren't *legal*," I corrected him, my teeth clenched so tightly that my jaws hurt. "But what you did to me certainly wasn't ethical."

"Now wait a minute, Ms. Gilbert. You're making some pretty serious charges."

"As far as I'm concerned, what you did is serious."

"And just what is it you think I did?"

"I don't *think*, I *know*. You jacked up your

estimate of the repairs I need done and made me believe the house is about to fall down around my ears. You wanted me to panic and sell it, after which you could pick it up for a song."

To my surprise, a half-guilty, half-embarrassed look appeared on his strong features. I hadn't expected that, and felt a little taken aback.

"You've got it all wrong," he told me. "Why don't you come in and sit down, and we can talk this over like civilized people." He waved toward the arched entrance to the living room.

I was still too angry to feel civilized, and I shook my head. "I don't see anything to talk over. I just wanted to let you know I'm aware of what you were up to."

He let out his breath and his well-shaped mouth tightened. "Will you stop all the melodrama?" he demanded. "I'm not up to anything. I admit I gave you a high estimate. But I didn't do it for the reasons you seem to believe."

"What other reasons could you possibly have?" I demanded in disbelief. "You don't even *know* me."

He gave me a very odd look. "Oh, yes, I do. I feel as if I've known you for a long time."

"What on earth are you talking about? The first time I ever laid eyes on you was at Aunt Edith's services."

The odd look intensified. "Edith and I were friends. She was always singing your praises. To her, you could do no wrong. She was so proud of you." His eyes bored into mine. His tone had made it clear that he didn't share my aunt's views.

I felt my face reddening, and wished my fair skin wasn't so prone to showing my feelings. "What does that have to do with anything?" I finally asked.

"I listened to that nice old lady talk about you — the wonderful niece — who didn't care enough about her to ever visit. Not once, not even when her health got so bad. Not until she died and left everything she had to you." His voice was flat and cold.

I stared at him, my anger gone, and feeling my face turn from red to icy pale. I understood now why he'd given me those cold looks at the services, and why he still resented and disliked me. He'd neatly turned the tables on me and put *me* on the defensive.

"I didn't know she had heart trouble," I finally said. "She never told me. We talked often on the phone and exchanged letters. She always said everything was fine with her."

I paused as the guilt swept over me again. "I know I should have visited her, and I planned to, but somehow the time just passed, and . . . and then it was too late." I pressed my lips together and looked away from him. I didn't want him to think I was trying to play on his sympathy.

There was a long silence. When I glanced at him again, he was staring at me intently, but I was surprised to see a softer expression on his face.

"It looks as if we both had some wrong ideas about each other," he said with a wry smile. "I didn't give you a high estimate. I honestly can't work for less. But I was trying to make things difficult for you, since I thought your only interest in the house was to fix it up and sell it at a profit."

"Why did you think I moved all the way here from L.A. if I was going to turn around and sell the house?"

He shrugged. "Because it needs a lot of repair and you couldn't handle all the details from out there."

"That may be true, but I moved here because I want to live in Cedar Grove. I wasn't aware the house was in this bad a shape until I moved in."

He gave me a look of disbelief. "You moved all the way across the country without knowing what you were getting into?" He shook his head. "City people."

I took a deep breath and let it out. "Look, Mr. Meade, I may be a city person now, but I lived in Cedar Grove until I was fourteen. I didn't want to move away then. I've always liked the town."

"Then why did you wait until your aunt left you her house to move back?" he asked.

"I don't think that's any of your business," I told him flatly. "Good-bye, Mr. Meade." I turned to leave. He was impossible. And just when I'd thought he was going to turn out to be halfway nice too.

"Wait," he said, sounding now as if he were annoyed with himself. "Don't go. You're absolutely right and I'm sorry."

I turned to find him actually smiling at me. As I hesitated, he stuck out his hand and said, "How about if we start all over? You can stomp my feet if I get out of line again."

His frank apology melted my anger. I looked at him for a moment, then gave him my hand. "All right, but I stomp pretty hard." The same as yesterday, I was much too aware of how his big, warm hand swallowed mine and made tingles run up my arm. I withdrew my hand and stepped back a little.

"But we may not have time to do much starting over," I said. "I'm afraid I'll have to sell the place as is."

"Do you really want to sell it?"

"You know I don't," I said a little impatiently. "I just told you I want to live here."

He hesitated a moment before saying, "I have a proposition to offer you, if you'd rather not sell."

My heart leaped with hope. I had no idea what he had in mind, but I'd listen to anything that might allow me to keep the house. "What is it?"

"You have about eight acres of good pastureland," he told me. "I have two horses that I've been boarding on the other side of town. It would be a lot more convenient for me to have them closer. If you're willing, I'll exchange my labor on the house for your letting me pasture my horses in your fields."

Hope sang in my veins now. This sounded too good to be true. Then I thought of something. "There's an old barn out back, but I'm afraid it's in worse shape than the house."

"No, it isn't. I looked it over a few weeks ago. It just needs a little patching up. Edith and I discussed the same arrangement I'm offering you, but she died before we could make definite plans."

I let out my breath, feeling relief flow through me. I gave him a wide smile and stuck my hand out again. "Then you've got a deal! I just hope you know what you're getting into."

He took my hand and held it a little longer than necessary. His eyes stared into mine. "I do know what I'm getting into, Dana Gilbert," he assured me. Then he released my hand and stepped back a little.

"Well, good," I said briskly, feeling my heart flutter a little. There was something in his tone that made me think he wasn't referring only to our swapping agreement. That thought made me distinctly uneasy. But it also gave me a sense of excitement.

But caution was going to be my middle name from now on, I reminded myself. I'd been burned once, and I had no intention of letting it happen again.

And it was the height of conceit to think that Jordan Meade had any plans to get involved with *me*. Just because I thought I'd read something into his words and tone a moment ago didn't necessarily mean that at all. Because I'd heard something else in his deep, pleasant voice: the same wariness that I felt. Maybe Jordan had also gotten burned a time or two.

"I'll start on the roof in the morning, if that's all right with you," he said. "I'm beginning a project in Virginia soon, but I have a little free time now that I've finished this house. Your roof should be done before we have another hard rain."

"The sooner the better," I answered. "And you can bring your horses any time you want."

"I'll do that in a few days. The roof is more important."

As I drove back up the road, I knew that I was going to be involved with Jordan, no matter what I was telling myself. We hadn't discussed just what repairs he would do, but it sounded as if he had more plans than just the roof. He was going to be around for a while. Not to mention the fact that with his horses pasturing on my land, he'd be around even longer. That didn't need to concern me, though, I assured myself. And besides, I remembered, he'd mentioned starting a new project soon. So that meant he'd have to get my repairs finished in a hurry.

We could keep this strictly a business arrangement, if we wanted to. *I* certainly did, didn't I? And he did too, didn't he? I parked and went inside the house to be greeted by a ravenous Smoke. I scooped him up and rubbed his arching back.

"Yes, I know, you're starving and won't last another fifteen minutes."

As I rummaged in the refrigerator for his food, I tried to push down the little voice inside my head that was asking me if I really believed that Jordan and I could keep things on a business level. And if I really wanted to.

Chapter Three

"I can't believe it," Lynn told me, her eyes wide. She propped her elbows on the post office window ledge. "Jordan Meade is going to be at your house for days at a time? And you're going to be *with* him?"

I looked up from my mail and frowned at her. "No, I'm not going to be with him. I'm going to be in my office typing, I hope." Not for anything would I admit that I'd entertained a few ideas like that myself.

She gave a long, mock sigh. "You've been here less than a week and already you've got the most eligible man in town — or the county, for that matter — interested in you."

"Lynn! I told you he's going to board his horses at my place in exchange for the work he does."

Lynn grinned. "I can see it now — the two of you riding off into the sunset together."

"That would be an unlikely sight, since I haven't been on a horse in years."

"Better and better. He can give you riding lessons." She beamed at me. "And the two of you can double-date with Cliff and me."

I shook my head and stuffed my mail into my tote bag. "Want to go to the movies with me tomorrow night? Or does Cliff keep you fully occupied?"

"Nope. We're just good friends. Sure, I'd love to."

I drove home, enjoying the early-summer sun and clear blue skies. Jordan had spent the morning working on the roof and had left for lunch a few minutes ago. After debating with myself whether to offer him a sandwich, I had decided not to. He might think — well, I didn't know what he might think, but I didn't want him to get the wrong idea. The farthest thing from my mind was encouraging anything more than friendship between us. *Oh, sure it is,* a little voice in my mind said. But I ignored it.

The phone was ringing as I let myself in. I hurried to the kitchen and grabbed it. Five minutes later I hung up and let out a sigh of relief. I had my first typing job! I hadn't expected anything so soon, because the summer term at the college had just started, but this was a high school student who had to make up work in summer school.

Smoke wrapped himself around my ankles, announcing he hadn't had his lunch yet. I fed him and fixed myself a sandwich. As we were finishing, I heard Jordan's truck pull up outside, and in a minute the hammering on the roof began again.

I should have asked him if he wanted to have lunch with me. After all, the bargain we'd struck was weighted heavily in my favor and both of us knew it. I would make a pitcher of iced tea and offer him some in a little while, I decided. And why not also offer him some of the brownies I'd baked yesterday? Most men loved brownies.

I heard a knock on the door and went to answer it. It was the student with his typing work. I got right to it, and worked for an hour and a half while the steady sound of Jordan's hammer kept on over my head. Finally, I decided to take a break. I put the tea and brownies on the kitchen table and went out the back door and over to Jordan's ladder.

He was straddling the ridgepole while he wiped his forehead with a handkerchief. He looked tired and warm. He also looked muscular and handsome in his jeans and white T-shirt — but that was none of my concern, I reminded myself.

"Want to take a break?" I called up to him. "I have some iced tea and brownies."

His head swiveled round and he gave me a quick glance and then a smile. "That sounds great. Be right down."

A few minutes later we were sitting across the table from each other. I really liked that cleft in his chin, I decided. It gave him a sort of Cary Grantish look.

Jordan finished half his tea, then put the glass down. "Just what I needed. These look good too. Did you make them?" He took a brownie and bit into it.

"With the help of Duncan Hines. I'm a confirmed chocoholic."

"So am I." He finished his first one and took another.

I felt gratified even if it had been a mix. I reached for one also, and then, with no warning whatsoever, Smoke leaped onto Jordan's lap and batted at his brownie with a small paw, causing him to drop it on the floor.

"Smoke! You get down from there this minute!" Now that he'd achieved his objective, the kitten obeyed readily. "I'm sorry," I told Jordan.

He grinned at me and helped himself to a replacement. "That's all right. I'm used to cats. My mother always has at least one, and usually more than that."

"Does your family live near here?" I asked. For some reason, Lynn, the fount of all news, hadn't given me this information. I was surprised to see his jaw muscle tighten when I asked him about his family.

He didn't answer for a moment. "In Philadelphia — the whole clan," he finally said. His voice sounded a little strained. "Mom and Dad and my brothers and their families. They keep trying to talk me into moving back there."

Was that the problem? I wondered. "I envy you your family," I told him. "I'm an only child."

"You must have been lonely at times." He polished off the brownie and reached for his tea again. "After Los Angeles, Cedar Grove must be awfully small and quiet."

There seemed to be a question in his voice. It was almost as if he couldn't believe that I really liked the town, and I remembered the things he'd said yesterday. I shrugged, determined to keep this conversation light and casual.

"That's why I moved here. No smog, no congestion. Also, it's a lot cheaper to live here than in L.A."

His stare turned into a smile. "That's true." He pushed back his chair and stood up. "Better get back to the roof. It's supposed to rain again tomorrow, and I'd like to have the worst of it repaired by then."

I hesitated, then asked, "Do you need some help? I almost fell off the roof the other day, but maybe I'd have better luck this time."

His smile widened into a grin. "In that case, I think you'd better stay on the ground. No, I don't need your help today. When I start on the chimney in the attic, then I will."

Relief filled me. I had no desire to get on that roof again. "Chimney?" I asked. Jordan had looked over the house this morning before he started on the roof, but he hadn't filled me in yet on what other repairs were needed.

"It has to have quite a few bricks replaced. And it would be unsafe to use any of the fireplaces the way they are now."

"Oh, I didn't know. Good thing it's summer and I didn't try to build a fire."

"Yes, it is. Thanks for the snack." He lifted his hand and headed out the back door again. It would be cozy in the attic with just the two of us. I could hand Jordan the bricks and he could putty them in, or whatever it was you did with bricks. I gave my head a shake. What was the matter with me?

I went back to work. Sitting at the typewriter with term papers would soon get rid of that kind of nonsense.

"So, how are the home renovations

coming along?" Lynn asked as we stood in line for tickets at Cedar Grove's only movie house. She gave me an arch look.

I gave her a bland smile in return. "Fine. Jordan finished the worst of the roof yesterday, since it was supposed to rain today. Which it didn't." I didn't add that Jordan planned to start on the chimney tomorrow. But no doubt she'd have it out of me before the evening was over.

"Has he brought his horses over yet?"

We paid for our tickets and then headed inside, where the wonderful aroma of buttered popcorn filled the air.

"No. But I think he plans to soon."

"You know that Jordan plays the saxophone in the town band," Lynn said as we looked for seats while juggling sodas and brimming bags of popcorn. "Where do you want to sit? Cliff always gives me a hard time for getting too close."

"Let's compromise with halfway down." I gave her a look as we settled ourselves. "Town band? I didn't even know there was one." I pictured Jordan playing the saxophone. For some reason, the idea tickled me.

"The band is fairly new — about five years, I think. But it's very popular. They play at the pavilion on Saturday nights, just like the school band used to. Cliff plays drums," she added. "Would you like to go this Saturday? I nearly always do."

Jordan was a man with many sides, I realized.

"That sounds like fun," I said, "and not just because Jordan plays saxophone."

"Of course not." She gave me a smug smile.

I decided we'd talked enough about Jordan. "I got two typing jobs already." The second client had called this morning, and instead of a student it was a businessman with overflow work. He'd asked me if I would work in his office a couple of mornings a week, but since I didn't want to do that, I'd talked him into letting me do the work at home.

"Maybe you should have accepted his offer," Lynn said. "It might lead to a permanent job."

"No, I want to teach. I just hope I get the position that's opening up in December."

"Better you than me. I like kids, but I wouldn't have the patience to teach them."

"It's a satisfying job. I like second graders best. They've already learned the basics but they're still young enough to think you know everything. If I get this job in January, it'll be first graders. I think I'll find that a challenge."

We enjoyed the movie, a comedy. Later we had a snack at Willard's Drive-In, still the favorite hangout of the high school crowd.

"See you Saturday, then?" Lynn asked as we left. "At the band concert?"

"All right. What time?"

"About eight. By the way, most women dress up a little — you know, skirt or dress instead of jeans." Lynn smiled at me and impulsively gave me a hug. "I'm glad you moved back here, Dana."

I hugged her back, feeling warmed by her words. "So am I," I told her, and knew that it was true, even if I did have to contend with a house needing repairs, lack of money, and the prospect of maybe not getting a job come winter.

And Jordan Meade, my inner voice added. *Don't forget about him. He's another reason you're glad you're here.*

I couldn't deny that, even though I wanted to.

"Just keep adding water until the mortar is thick enough to spread," Jordan told me, stirring the mix in the big pail with a trowel. We'd laid newspapers on the wood planks of the attic floor.

"Kind of like making mud pies," I said.

"What if I don't get it right?"

He shrugged. "No big deal. If it's too thin, we just add more mortar. And if too thick, more water. Just keep on stirring to prevent it from setting."

He picked up some of the bricks he'd brought this morning and smeared mortar along the sides.

"These bricks should match the old ones pretty well. They do a good job with the antique-brick reproductions these days."

"Does it matter? It's just the attic," I said as I kept on stirring the whitish mix in the pail.

He gave me a kind of dark look as if I'd disappointed him somehow. "I try to do a job as well as I can."

I watched his well-shaped, skillful hands fit a new brick into the gaping holes in the big chimney where he'd removed the crumbling, old ones. Feeling as if he'd reproved me, I said, "I just meant that they must cost more." I hated to think what all this was going to cost.

"I got a good price on them," he said after a moment. He turned and held out his hand.

I handed him another brick and our fingers touched. Mine were cold and with a dab of mortar on my thumb. His were warm and firm. It felt good. But I ignored that and wondered exactly what he meant by a good price. Jordan was always evasive when I asked about expenses, saying he'd give me a bill for the materials when he finished.

And I hadn't told him about the water heater yet. The situation was worsening. This morning I'd taken a cold shower, which I don't like even in the summer. Besides, it was a pain having to heat all my dishwater. I cleared my throat as I handed him another brick. "I hate to bring this up, but my water heater seems to have conked out too."

He gave me a quick look and shook his head. "Are you beginning to wish you'd stayed in L.A.?"

There he went again with the assumption that I couldn't stick it out, that I was a city girl at heart. "No," I said, annoyed. "I don't. And I wish you'd stop saying those things."

He gave me another look, which changed into a grin. "Today the water heater, tomorrow the furnace," he said. "I'll take a look at it this afternoon."

After a moment I smiled back, a little reluctantly. Maybe I was just letting his teasing remarks get to me. Probably he didn't mean anything by them. And I had to keep in mind that this was only a business arrangement between us. But I still felt as if I were getting much the better end of the bargain. Which reminded me of something. "When are you going to bring your horses over?" I asked.

He fitted another brick in place before he answered. "I thought maybe Saturday. I was wondering if you'd like to come with me and ride one of them. That way, I wouldn't have to trailer them over."

My heart sank. "I don't think so. I haven't ridden a horse since I was a kid."

He gave me one of his raised-eyebrow looks. "If you can sit on a merry-go-round horse, you can ride Sally. Placid is her middle name."

I chewed my bottom lip. I did owe him, no getting around it. "How far would it be?" I finally asked.

"Just across town. We could take back roads, where there wouldn't be much traffic. Not that Sally or Ranger spook at traffic."

"All right. But I reserve the right to change my mind if I get up on Sally and she realizes I don't know what I'm doing."

"We could go over tomorrow so you could get used to her," Jordan said. "These few days off are going to spoil me. When the

Virginia project gets going, I'll have to spend most of my time there."

I looked at him, wishing this arrangement could last longer. "You call all this work taking time off?" I asked him.

"Yep. I enjoy restoring old houses. It isn't work to me."

"You could have fooled me." I grinned. "But then, I'm a 'city person.' "

He gave me a wry grin in return. "Maybe there's hope for you yet. You're a good mason's helper."

"Thanks — I guess. I have some typing to do tomorrow morning for Mr. Hadley," I went on. "But I should be done with it by noon."

"Good," he said. "I wanted to ask you something else. Would you mind feeding and watering the horses when I'm in Virginia?"

"Of course not," I answered quickly. "I'm getting the better end of this bargain, anyway."

"There, see how easy it is?" Mounted on his big bay gelding, Jordan was close beside me. "Just hold the reins loosely. Sally has a very soft mouth and she obeys easily."

"Whatever you say," I mumbled, wishing the knot in my stomach would go away. I tried to relax, telling myself he was right. Sally, a pretty gray mare, didn't seem to mind me on her back in the slightest. I followed Jordan as we rode slowly around the big field. After a few minutes the knack of it started to come back to me, and I relaxed a little and even began to enjoy it.

I was going to be sore tomorrow, but so what? I'd get over it. After an hour of practice Jordan stopped the horses. "You really haven't ridden for a long time?" he asked. "That's hard to believe. You sit the horse well. You have a natural seat."

I felt warmed by his compliment. "My seat is going to wish I hadn't done this tomorrow," I answered. "One of my school friends had a horse when we lived here. I used to ride quite a bit."

"What do you say we take the horses today instead of waiting until tomorrow?"

I swallowed, then lifted my shoulders. I was sure that Jordan wouldn't suggest this unless he thought I could do it safely. "Okay by me."

An hour later we came out of a patch of woods and onto Harris Road. I felt exhilarated by the ride, but relieved we were nearly home. Home. I rolled the word around on my tongue. It sounded great. I really felt this way about Aunt

Edith's house, I realized.

And a lot of that feeling was due to the man riding beside me, I had to admit. He wore his usual jeans and T-shirt, this one dark blue, with the addition of calf-high boots. He rode very well, and it was a pleasure to watch him.

He looked up and caught my glance and smiled. "Almost there," he said. "Are you tired?"

"Not really. But I don't want to think about tomorrow. I probably won't be able to get out of bed."

"Take a long hot bath tonight," he advised. "That will head off the worst of the aches."

"Yes, I will." With a rush of pleasure I remembered that that would now be possible, because Jordan had replaced a burned-out heating element in my water heater yesterday. It was wonderful to have plenty of hot water again.

"Why do you have two horses?" I asked Jordan as we reached the field alongside the house. "I mean, Sally isn't exactly the kind of mount I'd think you'd choose, even though she is pretty."

He gave me a quick smile. "You're right. About next year, Sally is going to produce a beautiful foal for me, I hope."

Jordan dismounted, opened the gate, and led his horse inside. I followed him, and then we led the horses to the small barn and took off their saddles and bridles. Jordan had made the repairs yesterday evening. "Is Sally expecting now?" I asked.

Jordan smiled at my unhorsey terminology. "No, not yet. But I'm planning to breed her before fall."

"What are you going to do with the foal?" I asked as we turned the horses out to graze. "Sell it?"

"I'm not sure yet."

"Maybe *I* could buy it," I blurted without thought, and then was appalled at myself. I didn't even have a job yet, and here I was talking about buying horses.

"Maybe you could," Jordan said after a moment.

He was now hanging the saddles over the racks he'd set up and the bridles upon hooks on the walls. As he turned and looked at me, our gazes locked and held. A shiver went down my spine. It was somehow a very intimate look, more so than a kiss might be, I thought. I felt very close to him. Did Jordan feel that way too? I wondered. Then he broke the look, turned away, and focused his attention on arranging a bridle strap on a hook.

"That is, if you decide to stay here," he added. His voice had changed; it was cool and a little distant now.

My happy mood fled. "I have every intention of making Cedar Grove my home," I answered stiffly. I turned away to stand in the doorway, wincing as a twinge of pain hit my back.

There was a silence, then Jordan walked up beside me. "We'll see." His voice was still cool. "You haven't been here very long yet."

"Long enough to know I want to stay." I didn't look at him, but in spite of my bewilderment, I was very much aware of him and his closeness.

"I'd better be getting home," he said after a moment. "Sally and Ranger seem to be settling in well. I don't think you'll have any problems, but if you do, I'm just down the road and you have my telephone number."

We walked back to the house in silence, but not a restful silence. The tension coming from Jordan was almost tangible.

At the house, I didn't ask Jordan in, as I'd halfway planned to do. He waved casually at me as he walked down the road to his house. As I watched his tall, well-built figure stride down the road, a sudden flash of insight hit me. Maybe that look we'd exchanged had affected Jordan the same way it had me. Could that be why he'd changed so abruptly? I knew that he was just as wary as I about getting involved. More so, maybe.

So he's smarter than you are, I told myself. *He's backing off before anything starts between us.* Well, there was no reason why we couldn't be friends. And that was obviously as far as Jordan wanted things to go. And I felt the same way, didn't I?

I knew the answer even as I tried to deny it. No matter how much I tried to convince myself otherwise, I *did* want to get further involved with him.

Chapter Four

"Good thing I remembered to tell you to bring a lawn chair," Lynn remarked as we settled ourselves on the grass in front of the pavilion on Saturday night.

"Yes," I agreed, looking around with pleasure. It was like going back in time. All the women wore pastels or bright summer clothes, and the men were in sports shirts and dress slacks, including the band members. I could almost believe that this was fifty or more years ago if I didn't look too closely.

Lynn nudged me. "There's Jordan. Doesn't he look great?"

She didn't have to point him out to me. I'd seen him first thing. She was right about his looks, but I wasn't going to admit that to her. Her match-making attempts were bad enough already. "So does everyone else," I said. "Cliff is good-looking too."

Lynn sighed and shook her head at my obvious attempts to change the subject. "Yes, he is."

I was surprised at the size of the town band, and a few minutes later, when they broke into a rousing Sousa march, I was also more impressed by their skill. I didn't know much about music, but instead of a bunch of amateurs, as I'd expected, these were real musicians who took what they did seriously.

Just then, Jordan looked right at me and then his eyes widened in surprise. I gave him a big smile, just as if we hadn't parted on cool terms Thursday.

Actually, I was surprised to see him here, because he'd phoned Friday to tell me he had to go to Virginia about his project there. Naturally, I hastened to assure him I didn't expect him to devote all his time to repairing my house, and that I'd take care of the horses during his absence. He then said he'd be over on Monday to finish the chimney, which left me wondering if he was sorry he'd gotten into this and was trying to back off.

I didn't know, but I decided now, as I listened to him expertly coax euphonious sounds from his saxophone, that I'd have a frank talk with him on Monday and tell him that I had never expected him to spend a lot of time on the repairs to Aunt Edith's house. I supposed that I would always think of it that way, even though I felt at home there now. It had been my aunt's house a lot longer than mine.

"Who's that?" Lynn suddenly asked me,

breaking my train of thought. "That older man on the end of the row ahead of us."

Glancing to where she indicated, I saw a nice-looking man who appeared to be in his late sixties. "How would I know?" I asked Lynn. "Remember, I haven't lived here for years."

"Oh, yeah, I keep forgetting that." She grinned at me. "It already seems like you've never left. Anyway, I've never seen him before, and I know everyone in town, I think."

I thought so too. Without being in the least offensive about it, Lynn was highly interested in people. "Maybe he's a newcomer and unattached," I said lightly. "We should find out and introduce him to Blythe."

"Hey, that's not a half-bad idea! Blythe has been rattling around in that big old house for years, ever since her husband died."

"She does seem lonely," I said. "And she loves to cook and bake for people. If I didn't want to, I'd never have to cook at all. She's always bringing me something."

Lynn bit her lip and tapped her fingers on her chair arm, already deep in thought. Then she looked at me, her eyes sparkling with mischief. "After this is over, I'll go tell him I'm head of Cedar Grove's welcoming committee and find out all about him."

"I didn't know Cedar Grove *had* a welcoming committee."

"It doesn't, but hey, why not form one? I'll be chairman and you're my first appointee."

"You're impossible, Lynn."

She gave me a superior smile and then began looking around the audience. In a minute she turned back to me, her smile even broader. "Guess who's sitting in back of us."

"Don't tell me — Blythe," I answered. I was getting caught up in the outrageous idea, and I couldn't resist glancing back. Blythe wore a pretty pink dress and was talking a mile a minute to a woman of about her own age. Blythe was an attractive and very nice woman. And she *did* seem lonely — she was always talking about how much she missed her husband. Maybe. . . . But I caught myself up short.

"Wait a minute," I told Lynn — "Are we crazy? We don't know anything about this new guy. He could be married — or Jack the Ripper's great-grandson, for all we know."

"I told you I was going to find out," Lynn said. "Relax."

I settled back in my seat, deciding to

enjoy the concert and leave the machinations up to Lynn. I was sure she was expert at them.

By the end of the concert, I was even more impressed with the caliber of the performers. Their range was broad, extending from marches to current songs to old sentimental tunes, and they were good at everything they played.

"Listen," Lynn said to me as the final selection started. "I was going to suggest you and Jordan come with Cliff and me to eat somewhere. So why don't you go arrange that while I pounce on the Mystery Man before he escapes?"

"I can't do that!" I told her, but as the band finished with a flourish, she gave me a brilliant smile and headed purposefully toward Blythe's future beau.

I would just ignore her idea of making up a foursome and get in my car and go home, I told myself. I glanced up at the bandstand and saw Jordan looking my way again. He gave me a little wave and a smile.

While I hesitated, I saw Lynn wave at Cliff and point to me. My heart sank. Oh, no, she must already have discussed this with him. My hunch was confirmed when Cliff smiled and waved at me and then headed for Jordan.

He said something to Jordan, and Jordan looked at me again, then back at Cliff, and nodded. I felt totally mortified. Now Jordan would think I'd been in on the idea, that I'd helped rig this up. I felt my face burning.

Lynn had reached her target and was talking to him animatedly. I hastily folded my lawn chair and made my way to the end of the row. I would explain my departure to her tomorrow.

"What's the hurry?" a familiar voice asked almost in my ear. The voice had a teasing note.

I swallowed, turned to Jordan, and pasted a bright smile on my face. His eyes were dancing and his mouth was curving upward just a little. He was carrying his saxophone case.

"Oh, hello, Jordan." My voice was as bright as my smile and just as phony. "I enjoyed the concert. The band is very good."

"We have a lot of fun," he said. "Cliff was telling me that he and Lynn were going out to eat, and they wanted to know if you and I would like to go too."

I felt my face grow even warmer, and decided to drop all the innocent stuff and be completely honest. "Look, Jordan, this was all Lynn's idea. She sprang it on me about five minutes ago. Sorry."

His dark brows arose in that quizzical way he had. "What are you sorry about? I think it's a great idea."

I blinked, not expecting this answer. "You do?" I asked lamely, shifting my lawn chair under my arm.

"Yes, I do," he said firmly. "Here, let me take that chair."

"It's not heavy and you already have your sax case," I protested. "I can manage it fine."

"I'm sure you can, but this has put me in a nostalgic mood —"

As he waved at the surroundings, I knew that he shared my feeling of being transported to an earlier time.

"To an age when women were sweet and helpless," he continued, grinning at me. "And men were gallant."

I couldn't help grinning back, and I surrendered the chair. "Maybe they were on to something," I said.

"I wouldn't be surprised." He held the chair easily with his unoccupied hand. "Well, are you going to disappoint Lynn and Cliff and me, or will you agree to come with us?"

"When you put it like that, how could I refuse?" I asked lightly. "Sure, I'll come."

"Good! Let's go to your car and I'll stow this away for you."

"All right." I turned to glance at Lynn, who was now leading the stranger purpose-fully toward Blythe. She caught my eye and winked, and then mouthed that she'd join me in a minute. I had a feeling that Blythe's single days were numbered.

"This is nice." I looked around the dining room of the country inn a few miles out of Cedar Grove.

Jordan sat at my left at the round table. "Is this a new place? I don't remember it from when I lived here."

"It's a few years old," Lynn answered. She took a sip of her water, then gave me a look like the cat that just got the canary. No wonder. She'd pulled off this double date and introduced the stranger to Blythe Cole, all within a few minutes.

"What's his name?" I asked her, knowing she'd pick up on whom I meant.

"Thomas Parker," she answered promptly. "And he's a widower too, and just moved to town. He and Blythe hit it off at once. They both love to garden."

Jordan gave both of us quizzical looks, and Cliff laughed as he said, "I always tell Lynn she should have been a marriage counselor. She just loves to get people to-gether."

Lynn gave him a pert smile. "What's the harm in that? People need other people. I stand firmly by that."

"That's true," Jordan put in, smiling at Lynn.

I couldn't help but notice that his glance at her was admiring, as well it should be — Lynn was very pretty in her blue dress and with a white flower tucked over her ear. I ignored the pang of something or other that assaulted me. Lynn had said that she and Cliff were only friends, and if Jordan was getting interested in her, that was fine with me. Just *fine*. And that would for sure get her off my back.

Jordan turned and caught me looking right at him, with I didn't know what kind of expression on my face. I hastily turned my attention to the menu and didn't look his way again until we'd all made our selections of beverage and dessert. Death by Chocolate was the dessert I picked, and so did Jordan. Lynn and Cliff chose cheesecake, with Lynn cheerfully remarking that we could share.

I pushed down a pang of regret that Jordan and I were having the same thing and couldn't share. I really had to get control of my thoughts and feelings, I decided. I'd never met a man before who could affect me as Jordan did. He had me running the emotional gamut from highs to lows in the space of a few minutes. It was unsettling, I didn't like it — and I would stop it.

An hour later, in the parking lot, I was spared the embarrassment of Jordan's having to offer to take me home, because we hadn't come together. Lynn got into Cliff's car and they made a hurried exit, obviously to leave Jordan and me alone. I was going to have a talk with her.

Jordan opened my car door for me. I got in and looked up at him. "This has been a nice evening."

"Yes, it was," he said, not moving away as quickly as I'd expected. "I'd like to do it again. Would you be interested?"

"What? In going to the band concert?" I asked, stalling for time while I thought over his offer. Did I want to go out with Jordan? I wasn't sure. I put my key into the ignition, giving him a casual glance. "Sure. I'll probably go most Saturday nights."

"That's nice, but it wasn't what I meant, and you know it. Would you like to go out with me — just the two of us, I mean."

Yes and no. He had me flip-flopping again, and when I'd just vowed that I'd stop letting him have this effect on me. It didn't seem to be an *easy* thing to stop.

"Why, uh, yes, I guess so," I said. *Boy, that was such a gracious and mature answer*, I told myself, glancing at him again.

His dark eyes gleamed. "I love your enthusiastic acceptance." He reached over and ran his hand down my hair, finishing with a light touch on my neck that felt anything but light. "What's wrong, Dana? Are you telling me to get lost and I'm too dense to get the message?"

"No," I said quickly before I could stop myself. "That's not it at all. I —" I took a deep breath and decided to tell him exactly how I felt. Maybe he already knew. Those glances of his seemed to indicate he had a pretty good idea.

"I just ended a relationship that didn't turn out the way I thought it would," I said bluntly. "I decided I'd be very careful before getting involved with a man again."

Oh, no, that was too blunt. He'd only asked me to go out with him; he hadn't proposed marriage. I bit my lip. "Not that I mean we're getting involved," I floundered. "But I just wanted you to know how I felt."

I felt his hand on the back of my neck again. I had to turn to look at him. The expression on his face wasn't at all teasing, as I'd half expected.

"Oh, but I think maybe we *are* in danger

of getting involved, Dana," he said softly. He withdrew his hand from my neck and stepped back from the car. "And, to relieve your mind, I completely agree with what you said. I feel the same way. So that should make things a lot easier, don't you think?"

I swallowed, feeling more bumbling than ever. I'd always known that Jordan was at least as wary as I was. What had I been worried about? I nodded. "Yes, I suppose so."

"Good night, Dana. If you like, I'll follow you home since we live on the same road."

I took another deep breath and forced a smile. "You don't have to bother. Nothing to worry about in sleepy little old Cedar Grove. No bright lights or muggers. This isn't L.A.," I said flippantly. Then I put my hand over my mouth and widened my eyes. "Whoops, sorry. I forgot L.A. was a dirty word to you."

His mouth tightened for a minute, then relaxed into a wry grin. "Not just L.A.," he said. "Big cities in general. And you're absolutely right. For sure, this isn't L.A. I'll see you Monday." He turned and walked to his car without looking back.

I started my car and drove home, trying to figure out what was going on — how I felt, how Jordan felt, whether we were getting involved in a relationship or not. Maybe I'd changed my life-style to a simpler one, but if I got involved with Jordan, I knew instinctively it wouldn't be simple at all. He was the most complex, many-sided man I'd ever met.

So he'll never bore you, I told myself as I parked in the driveway. I let myself into the house, glad I'd left the porch light on. Smoke was ecstatic to see me after perhaps thinking I'd deserted him for good.

I scooped him up and caressed him, taking comfort in his loud, happy purrs. "Why can't everything be as uncomplicated as you are?" I asked him. "Life would be so much simpler."

Was that what I wanted: a simple, uncomplicated life with no surprises, nothing to unsettle me or shake me up? Of course I didn't. It would bore me silly.

With Lynn and Jordan in your life, I don't think you'll have to worry about that, I thought as Smoke and I headed upstairs. The comforting warmth as I stood under the shower a few minutes later reminded me again of how much I was letting myself get in Jordan's debt.

When I'd agreed to his plan, I hadn't realized how much time the repairs were going to take, or that new things, such as the water heater's conking out, were bound to happen. I would help him as much as possible, I decided, so that he wouldn't have to spend so much time here.

I tried to think of something else I could do to make our agreement more fair, but couldn't come up with anything except doing his housework and laundry, and that would be going a bit too far.

One thing I would do, though, was to give him lunch every day he was here working. Maybe I could cook dinner for him a couple of times a week too. No, I decided, dinner was also going too far.

As I shampooed my hair, the thought struck me that everything I was thinking of meant that Jordan and I would be together more.

And that will really improve the situation, won't it? I thought crossly.

Chapter Five

"You told Thomas Parker *what?*" I asked Lynn, passing her the plate of chocolate-chip cookies.

Lynn shrugged, not looking a bit repentant. She took two more cookies. "Well, maybe Blythe *is* having trouble with her roses. After all, anyone could." She grinned at me.

I sighed. "So that's why I saw Thomas out in the yard with her this morning. Now that you mention it, Blythe seemed to be pointing out something to him on the rosebushes."

Lynn took a bite of cookie. "Umm, these are scrumptious. Did you ever think of taking up baking as another way to bring in some extra money this summer?"

"No, I never have," I told her. "I'm merely an all-right baker, though I tend to lean heavily toward mixes. Blythe made these." I helped myself to another one.

"Blythe *is* really interested in him," Lynn insisted. "Because she's been president of the garden club for years, and knows everything there is to know about roses or anything else that grows, as well as being one of the best cooks in town."

"Do you really think she'd like to get married again?" I asked. "What if she's perfectly happy with her life?"

"Then why was she standing around in her rose garden with Thomas Parker?" Lynn asked logically.

"Probably because she's interested in him," I admitted. "Listen, Lynn, I want to talk to you."

"I'm all ears." She leaned back in one of Aunt Edith's maple chairs and looked at me expectantly.

"You know, what you did at the concert was really embarrassing. You made it appear I was trying to rope Jordan into asking me out."

Lynn gave the last bite of her second cookie to Smoke, who, sitting by her side, was giving her one of his I'm-dying-of-starvation looks.

"He didn't act to me as if he felt like that," Lynn said, grinning.

"Just the same, please don't do it again."

"I won't," she readily agreed.

"You won't?" I gave her a surprised look. Could it be this easy?

Her grin widened. "I won't have to. Because I betcha he asked you out again, didn't he?"

I opened my mouth to argue, then changed my mind and laughed. "You really are something else, do you know that?"

"That's what comes of being the only girl and having three older brothers. I learned how to outwit them early on because I couldn't outfight them. So tell me, did you accept?"

"I guess so," I told her.

It was Monday evening. Jordan had spent the early morning grooming and riding his horses, and I had spent it typing for Mr. Hadley, and thinking enviously of Jordan out in the fields.

Later, after we'd finished the chimney, Jordan said he had to go back to Virginia the next day. I wished he weren't going, but I told him not to worry about the horses. I enjoyed taking care of them.

Lynn now gave me an incredulous glance. "You *guess* he asked you out again?"

"I said I'd go out with him, but since I wasn't exactly enthusiastic about it, he didn't suggest a date. He didn't mention it today, either. Not that I care," I added hastily. "I'm in no hurry to start dating again."

"Not every man is a jerk like Bruce," Lynn told me.

"Of course not, but I'm still in no hurry."

"Listen, if Jordan Meade asked *me* out, believe me, I'd be enthusiastic."

I remembered the look that Jordan had given her Saturday night at the inn. "Are you interested in him?" I asked her. "Because if you are. . . ."

She gave me an incredulous stare. "Do you think I'd be pushing you two together if I were? I don't want anyone who's planning to spend the rest of his life in Cedar Grove. I've got larger horizons in mind."

"Well, there's nothing between Jordan and me," I insisted, even though I knew that it wasn't the exact truth. There *was* something between us. I just wasn't sure what it was. "Sometimes I don't even think he likes me much. He can act so odd and moody."

"If he didn't like you, he wouldn't have asked you out," Lynn said firmly. "Maybe there are other reasons for his moodiness. I've heard he was engaged to some Philadelphia society girl a year or so ago, and she dumped him."

"Jordan? I'd speculated that he'd been involved in a bad relationship, but. . . ."

Lynn nodded. "Although I find it hard to believe that any woman in her right mind would dump him."

Privately I agreed with her, but I wasn't going to say so. Instead I told her, "Maybe that's part of it. I don't think he gets along with his family very well, either. He said they're not happy he moved away from Philadelphia."

"So there you are. It probably has nothing to do with you."

After that positive note, I decided to change the subject, and we agreed to go to another movie on Wednesday night and to the band concert on Saturday.

Two days later I opened the door to Aunt Edith's bedroom and went inside with my cleaning supplies. Jordan was off to Virginia and I'd caught up on my typing jobs. I'd put this chore off long enough, but I still felt uncomfortable at the thought of going through all my aunt's belongings.

First I went to her closet, where I began to sort through the clothes. Most of the things were old and out of style but still serviceable. I would give them to one of the local charities, I decided.

Tears filled my eyes when I found a red woolen dress. I remembered that dress — she'd always worn it on Christmas Day. Quickly I took it off its hanger and folded it. Someone would get some use, even pleasure, out of it. Aunt Edith would like that.

By noon I'd packed the contents of the

closet and drawers into boxes. I'd kept Aunt Edith's garnet earrings and brooch and a gold locket that she'd worn a lot. Also an emerald-green scarf and a few other things that had sentimental value. I carried the boxes downstairs, left them in the living room for the time being, and then went back up to clean the room.

It wasn't hard to do, because Aunt Edith had been neat and tidy. But I decided that the big braided rug should be taken out to the backyard and hung over the line and beaten and aired. I rolled it up and carried it down, which was more of a job than I'd expected. I caught myself wishing I'd waited until Jordan came back. Good grief! He wasn't my personal handyman!

I tried to ignore the fact that Jordan didn't seem the least bit interested in following up on asking me out, and I concentrated on hoisting the rug over two of the clotheslines out back. Dust flew everywhere, and after a sneezing fit, I finished the chore and trudged back upstairs.

The rug must have been there a long time, because the wood beneath it was much lighter than the rest of the floor. I dust-mopped the floor and then started wet-mopping it. When my mop strings caught in a rough place on one of the boards where the rug had been, I leaned down to untangle it.

The floor was of wide-planked oak, and the mop was snagged on an edge that was higher than the others. On closer examination, however, I saw that a square had been cut in the floor and then neatly fitted back together.

My curiosity was aroused now, and I tugged at the protruding edge, which finally gave way. As I lifted it, I saw a compartment in the floor about a foot square. Then I drew in my breath, because the hiding place contained a packet of what looked like letters tied with a faded blue ribbon.

I stared at the packet for a long time. Undoubtedly, these letters had belonged to Aunt Edith. Did I have the right to take them out and read them? Would she mind? *No,* I finally decided, *she wouldn't.* She would have burned them years ago if she hadn't wanted to take this chance.

Carefully, I lifted the packet out and looked at it. The top envelope was addressed to Aunt Edith in a strong, masculine-looking script, its black ink still easily read. The name Paul Evans was written in the upper left-hand corner.

I took the packet to my room and put it into a dresser drawer for safekeeping. Then

I forced myself to finish my housecleaning, even though my curiosity was at fever pitch. I would read the letters this evening, I decided, and hurried through the rest of the work.

After an early dinner I showered and then got out the letters and took them to bed. Smoke batted an inquisitive paw at the blue ribbon as I untied it and carefully laid it aside.

I picked up the top envelope, opened it, took out the folded sheet of paper, which was dated nearly sixty years ago, and read:

Dear Edie,

This will be the last letter I'll be writing to you, because by this time tomorrow, we'll be together for always. You'll be Mrs. Paul Evans.

I know how much it upsets you that we have to elope, but your parents will never agree to our marrying. We can't let the bad blood between our families keep us apart when we love each other this much.

All my love,
Paul

I held the letter after I finished it and wondered what had happened afterward, because Aunt Edith hadn't married Paul or any other man. And I'd never heard this story from my parents.

I refolded the letter, and as I replaced it in the envelope, I saw something else in there — a yellowed newspaper clipping. I drew it out and my eyes filled with tears as I read of Paul's being killed in a house fire the very next day after writing the letter.

Had Aunt Edith waited for Paul to come for her, pacing the floor as the time dragged on and he didn't come? Or had she found out about his death from the newspaper? She must have loved him very much to have never married another man. And I was sure it wasn't because she'd never had any other offers. I'd seen pictures of her when she was young. She was very pretty, and she'd been a spirited, interesting woman all her life.

As I read through the rest of the letters in the packet, I wished I hadn't read the last letter first. It was like knowing the end of a story before you read the beginning.

Aunt Edith's and Paul's families had apparently been feuding for about a generation or so, for so long that no one was even sure what had started it. Since she was of age, she didn't need her parents' consent to marry, but I could imagine how she'd wanted it, anyway. Then to have her chance at happiness snatched from her the very day she was to marry Paul! It was heartrending.

An hour later I carefully replaced the blue ribbon around the letters and found a shoe box to put them in for safekeeping. Then I placed it on my top closet shelf.

I tried to go to sleep, but found myself staring at the dark ceiling while the sad and tragic story unreeled in my mind like scenes in a movie. Annoyed at my restlessness, Smoke gave me one of his discontented sounds and moved to the foot of the bed.

"Go ahead, desert me," I told him. "Just wait. I'll remember that tomorrow morning when you want your breakfast."

He ignored me, as cats do, and curled up and went instantly back to sleep. I gave him a dark look, wishing I had that ability.

At last, I gave up, turned the light back on, and reached for the pad of paper I always kept in my nightstand drawer. Maybe, if I wrote down the scenes playing themselves out in my head, they would quit tormenting me.

Finally, my cramping hands made me stop writing. I glanced at the clock, amazed to see it was two A.M. I hadn't been this engrossed in anything since my early college days, when I was a journalism major and had loved writing.

I'd switched my major to education after the first semester, when I decided it was a safer choice, and I believed that I'd put all desire to write behind me. Maybe that wasn't so, I thought now. Maybe it had only been suppressed, and was waiting for this moment, when an overwhelming interest would liberate it.

"Hand me that big crescent wrench, will you?" Jordan said as he lay stretched out under my kitchen sink in a very uncomfortable-looking position.

"Sure thing." I searched hurriedly through his toolbox, not wanting him to know the full extent of my ignorance. Then I saw the small wrench he had flung down in disgust a few moments ago.

Eureka! He must want a wrench like that one, only bigger. And there it was. As I laid it on Jordan's outstretched palm, the tips of my fingers touched his, and a small shiver went up my spine. With no warning, I found myself wishing he would throw down the wrench and pull me down beside him and kiss me. I felt my face burning and quickly straightened up, glad he hadn't been looking at me.

Jordan had come back from Virginia last night, and he'd called to say he wanted to fix the dripping faucets today. I hadn't argued, since that was part of our original agreement. It was pouring rain, a fitting day for the job at hand. This was the last one, thank goodness, and Jordan had already stopped the leak.

Now he was addressing the new problem that had developed last night: The sink was totally clogged. It hadn't responded at all to my attempts to clear it with a plunger and several applications of drain cleaner.

Jordan placed the wrench on the pipe joint and turned it, grimacing. Finally it gave, and he took the trap off, which, to my embarrassment, revealed the source of my troubles — an accumulation of food particles.

"It would help if you'd put this kind of stuff in the trash," he said, doing just that.

"I'm sorry. I had a garbage disposal in my apartment in L.A. and I keep forgetting."

The minute I'd said it, I wished I could take it back, because every time I mentioned L.A. it seemed to set Jordan off.

"Well, this isn't an apartment in L.A.," he said, a little curtly. "If you city people knew what you were getting into, you'd probably never move to small towns or the country. You have a septic tank here, not a modern city sewage system."

"You sound like this is the wilderness," I said crisply. "And I'm not exactly a city person. I lived the first fourteen years of my life here in Cedar Grove."

His face gradually relaxed into a smile. "It would have been better if you'd lived the *last* fourteen years here," he said.

I took a deep breath, then smiled back at him. "What was that you said about a septic tank?"

"If this one is new enough and large enough, you shouldn't have any problems." He put the trap back, stood up, and brushed dust from his jeans and shirt. "If not, you should have it pumped out once in a while."

My heart sank. "I don't even know where it's located, let alone how big or new it is."

"I can probably find it for you. The grass will be greener there and along the drain lines."

I bit my lip. Instead of diminishing, my problems seemed to be multiplying as time went on, and I couldn't keep letting Jordan do these things. "Thanks," I finally said. "I'm soon going to owe you pasture for your horses up to about the year 2000."

His smile was broader now. "Don't worry about it. I'm not spending that much time here, and, besides, I like to work on these old houses." He looked at me, then asked,

"Are you going to the Fourth of July parade?"

The question surprised me, because I knew he wasn't asking me to go with him. Lynn had already told me the town band would be marching in the parade. "Yes," I said. "I'm meeting Lynn downtown."

"How about going with me somewhere to eat afterward?"

Apparently he hadn't decided not to go out with me, after all. A small, warm glow started somewhere inside me. "What did you have in mind?"

"How about a picnic?" he asked, picking up his yellow slicker.

"That sounds like fun, but there's one condition. I want to supply the food."

"That depends. Can you fry chicken and make good potato salad?"

"No, but Colonel Sanders and the deli section of the supermarket will take care of it. Now, if you'd asked me to come up with a great chef's salad or a fruit dessert, that would be different. I'm used to eating light." I stopped myself before I mentioned that most people I knew in L.A. ate light.

"So am I, but all those calories and cholesterol won't hurt us once in a while." He put on the slicker. "I'll see you the day after tomorrow, then."

I watched him cross the backyard to his truck. I liked the way he moved — easily, in complete control of his body, and as if he knew exactly what he was doing and where he was going.

Smoke puffed as he wrapped himself around my ankles. I scooped him up and ran my hand down his back. He was growing up fast and soon wouldn't be a kitten anymore. That thought made me a little sad, but I knew I'd enjoy him as a grown-up cat too.

Everything in life changed, I reminded myself. And it looked as if my relationship with Jordan might be about to change too. I knew I was looking forward to the picnic and being alone with him.

I laughed at myself as I opened a can of cat food for Smoke. Jordan and I had been alone together for several hours today and at other times too. But that wasn't the same. Jordan kept everything on a business level when he was here, just as he should. But the picnic would be different.

I felt happy suddenly, as if good things were just around the corner. I wanted to get back to the slowly growing pile of typed pages I was working on in the evenings. Aunt Edith's tragic love story, with some liberal dollops of fiction from my imagination, was taking shape. I hadn't told anyone, even Lynn, about what I was doing, because I still could hardly believe myself I was doing it.

I'd forgotten the deep pleasure that writing always gave me, but it was coming back now, full strength. I didn't have the slightest idea what I was trying to do, but something inside me was compelling me to finish the story.

"All this and a picnic with Jordan too," I told Smoke. He agreed with me as he polished off his tuna dinner and asked for more.

Chapter Six

I stood beside Lynn on the sidewalk, the afternoon sun beating down on my back. Watching the parade, I again had that strange sense of being in another time. In addition to the usual drum majorettes and baton twirlers, there were several floats with people in period costumes depicting the history of Cedar Grove.

Then, of course, there was the town band, whose women wore long red skirts and white Gibson-girl blouses with blue bows. I smiled when I saw Jordan, dressed like all the other men in dark-blue trousers with a red-and-white striped shirt and bright-red suspenders. He gave a quick glance toward the spectators lining the sidewalk as he passed, and impulsively I waved at him. A warm feeling filled me when he waved back and smiled.

"I'm glad I brought my camera," I told Lynn after taking several pictures. "I wouldn't have missed this for the world."

She gave me a skeptical look. "Don't try to convince me that after living in Los Angeles all these years, with the Rose Bowl Parade and everything else that goes on out there, Cedar Grove's July Fourth celebration thrills you."

I frowned at her. "I wish you and Jordan would stop doing that. It's getting tiresome."

"Doing what?" Her eyes sparkled as always at any mention of Jordan. Not that I thought she was interested in him for herself — she was just in her normal matchmaking mode.

"Assuming that I'm some kind of big-city sophisticate. Why in the world do you think I moved to Cedar Grove if I don't like small-town life?"

"I can't imagine. I'd give anything to get away from here."

"What's wrong with Cedar Grove?" I asked her. "It's attractive, clean, quiet. You have a good job."

"Oh, it's a nice-enough town. It's just that I'd like to get away — see the world a little." She sighed. "Fat chance of that happening." She gave me another glance. "Jordan can't understand why you moved here? Now, that surprises me. He did the same thing — moved here from a big city, I mean."

"It beats me. But every time I mention L.A., he gets all bent out of shape and tells me I'm a city girl and I won't be able to stick it out here."

"Maybe he's teasing you."

"It's more than that."

"Give him time," Lynn advised. "After a while he'll see he's wrong."

"You're probably right," I said, and we turned our attention to the parade.

I'd told her about the picnic today, then wondered if she'd suggest that she and Cliff join us. But she hadn't. I'd been at once relieved and a little apprehensive, which was silly, because Jordan and I had been alone together a lot at my house. But that was kept strictly on a friendly, business footing.

"There's Blythe — and look who's standing beside her." Lynn's voice was heavy with meaning.

"It has to be Thomas Parker." I glanced down the street. Sure enough, Blythe, decked out in a pretty blue dress, was smiling at Thomas and talking a mile a minute. Thomas seemed to be listening attentively, occasionally putting in a few words himself.

"A match made in heaven," Lynn said smugly. "She talks and he listens. Aren't you glad we got them together?"

"What do you mean *we?* I had nothing to do with it."

"Oh, yes, you did. You gave me the idea in the first place."

"Maybe I did, but I had no intention of acting on it."

Lynn patted my arm. "That's the difference between you and me. You think up good ideas, and I act on them."

"Someday, you're going to act on something and get yourself in trouble."

"Maybe I will, but that might be fun too. I'm going to find Cliff and see if he wants to get something to eat. I'm starving."

The parade had wound to a close. "So am I. Jordan's picking me up at the house since I still have to get the chicken and potato salad."

We separated and I made my two stops, adding fresh fruit and some delectable-looking rolls to my purchases. I'd made a pitcher of iced tea this morning. Half an hour later, I felt a little flutter of anticipation in my stomach as I answered the door.

Jordan had changed into tan slacks and a blue shirt that enhanced his good looks. He glanced at my mint-green dress with approval as he entered, and I was glad I'd taken extra pains with my appearance.

"All ready!" I picked up the wicker basket I'd loaded with food and he took it from me. His hand briefly touched mine, and as usual I felt a tingle go up my arm. I wondered briefly why Bruce's touch hadn't elicited that response from me when I thought I was in love with him.

Jordan hadn't brought his truck today. No indeed. A Thunderbird convertible sat in front of the gate with its top down and its black paint glistening in the sunlight.

"I see houses aren't the only things you like to restore," I told him as he stowed the picnic hamper in the backseat. "This is gorgeous."

He smiled as he opened the passenger door for me. "Thanks, but I didn't do this myself. I love old cars, but I don't know anything about restoring them."

I ran my hand over the smooth leather of the front seat. "I've never ridden in one before, but I can see they might become addictive."

"You're right, they can." He got in beside me and turned the key. The powerful engine came to life and he drove smoothly down the country road. I had no idea where we were going, but I didn't care. I leaned back and let the breeze whip my hair around my face. Normally, I hate that, but today it felt good.

I glanced over at Jordan, who was concentrating on his driving. The sun struck glints off his black hair. His strong chin with that little cleft and his straight nose in profile made a little shiver go down my spine. I would have liked to move closer to him, maybe even lay my head on his shoulder. Of course I did neither. I adjusted my seat belt and admired the passing scenery.

"Where are we going?" I finally asked to break the silence. It wasn't an uncomfortable silence, at least not to me, but still it had gone on for quite a while.

As I looked at him, he gave me a quick glance, then smiled. "I was wondering when you'd ask that."

"This is so nice, I really don't care," I said, then wondered if he would think I was so glad to be with him that our destination didn't matter. Which was so close to the truth that I felt my face burning.

"I want to show you a special place," he said after a while.

"Fine," I answered. I couldn't tell from his tone if he'd picked up on my feelings. His voice sounded just the same, firm and deep and sure.

He turned at the next crossroads and took an even narrower road than the one we were on. This one wound itself deep into the country, into a valley where the hills spread around us in the distance, blue and beautiful.

We passed picture-postcard farms with

big red barns and stone farmhouses. Finally he turned into a lane where huge oaks and maples made a canopy overhead. The road curved, going steadily uphill, and then a big, stone, two-story house came into view on top of a rise. Jordan pulled up in front of the house and stopped.

I drew in my breath at the sheer beauty around me. "Jordan, this is fantastic!"

He gave me a warm smile. "I hoped you'd like it." He got out and retrieved the hamper from the backseat. "Where do you want to eat? We've got about a hundred acres to choose from." He waved his hand to encompass everything surrounding us.

I walked over to him. "Does all this belong to you?" I asked, my heart lifting at the spectacular panorama spread out all around us.

"Yes. I bought it just a few months ago. The house needs a lot of work inside, but I think this is going to be my home."

Something in the way he spoke made me look at him. His face was full of a possessive love as he looked around him. I could imagine him, a hundred and fifty years or so ago, when this house was built, standing here with pride of ownership in every strong line of his body and face. I could understand that fully. In fact, I felt some of it myself.

"It will be a wonderful place to live," I finally said. "As for where we eat — you choose. You know the place."

"Yes, I do," he answered, that possessive pride still in his voice. "There's an old orchard in back of the house. How about there?"

"That sounds nice."

Jordan got a blanket out of the trunk and gave it to me, and we walked behind the house, through the high and uncut grass, until we reached the orchard. It was neglected too, but the old trees retained a gnarled grace. At last he stopped at a big one with wide branches.

"This is my favorite tree," he said while I laid out the blanket under its shade and he set down the hamper. "It looks as if it's lived a long, happy life."

That seemed an oddly poetic turn of phrase for Jordan, who I'd always thought was supremely practical. But maybe he wasn't. It certainly wasn't especially practical to want to live way out here.

"I can see what you mean," I answered, looking at the old tree. It was full of deadwood needing to be cut out, and the trunk was covered with fungi, but it was still appealing.

He picked up something from the ground and handed it to me. "I don't know what kind of apples these are, but I don't think they're a hybrid. Hybrids weren't prevalent when this orchard was planted, and they're usually more perfectly shaped. But these might have a great taste."

The apple felt warm in my palm. It was small and green and a little misshapen, but maybe he was right. "I'd like to try them when they're ripe," I said, returning the apple with a smile.

"That's a date." He smiled back. "We'll have another picnic under this tree in a couple of months."

"Sounds like fun." I tried to ignore the way my heart had leaped at that remark, which seemed to promise that we were going to have some kind of future together. I opened the hamper and took out the small vinyl tablecloth and spread it out. Then I removed the food containers and the paper plates and utensils.

"I see you weren't kidding when you mentioned Colonel Sanders," Jordan remarked as I handed him the carton full of crisp, browned chicken.

"Nope. Why, did you think I was?"

"I wasn't sure. I thought maybe you were planning to bowl me over with your home cooking." He took a healthy bite, then grinned at me.

"Not me." I passed him the potato salad and rolls. "Supermarket special. However, I *did* make this iced tea with my own two hands." I poured him a glass from the thermos and handed it across.

"You make good iced tea, I know that. Maybe you can learn to cook in time." His voice was light and bantering.

I raised my eyebrows at that while pouring myself a glass. "I can cook, but I doubt if I'll ever cook like this."

"Not even if your husband has put in a long, hard day and needs the calories and comfort?"

Suddenly, his voice didn't sound so light anymore. I glanced at him. He was looking straight at me, a serious expression on his face. I felt a small prickle of awareness move down my back.

"I'm not at all sure I'm going to have a husband to worry about," I said in a moment, lowering my tea glass. "People don't need to get married in order to live happy, fulfilled lives." Why in the world was I saying these things? He hadn't asked me for my views on marriage. I lowered my head and concentrated on my food.

The silence drew out and I finally glanced at Jordan. His face was still serious and he was still looking at me. "That's true," he said finally. "Not all people need to be married. But you don't strike me as that type."

"What's that supposed to mean?" I asked flippantly, feeling a little edgy at the turn the conversation had taken. "That I can't take care of myself? I've been doing that since my parents died when I was eighteen."

"No, that's not what I meant. I'm sure you're quite able to take care of yourself. But you're also a very feminine woman." His voice held a strange blend of admiration and something I couldn't identify but that increased my edginess.

"Thanks, I think," I told him lightly. "Here, have some more chicken. How long have you lived in Cedar Grove?" I asked to change the subject.

"About three years." He took another piece of chicken and more potato salad.

"How did you happen to settle down here?" I persisted. If it was going to be question-and-answer time, I could ask some questions too.

He didn't answer for a while, and when he did, his voice had tightened. "My father owns a construction company, and my brothers and I have worked for him since we were teenagers. Dad tried to talk me into staying with the family business, but I wanted to branch out on my own. Maverick at heart, I guess."

He gave me a wry smile, and I remembered how he'd clammed up when I'd asked him about his family the other day. There had been some family fights about this decision, I'd bet.

"Anyway, I built a house for someone in Cedar Grove and liked the town. So I bought an old house there, restored and sold it, and then bought a couple more. It got to be too much trouble to drive back and forth to Philly all the time, and, besides, I decided I liked small-town life. There was plenty of work in the area and more houses I wanted to buy and restore, and so I stayed."

He spread out his hands, his smile wider. Obviously, he was trying to lighten things up. "That's the not-so-fascinating story of my life. What about yours?"

"I thought Aunt Edith had filled you in on me," I answered, making my voice casual. I handed Jordan a banana and peeled one for myself.

"She hit the high spots, but she never mentioned anything about your love life."

His own tone was as light as my own, but his words made my heart leap and beat faster. "I didn't know we were talking about love lives. What about your own?"

His face tightened again, as it had a

moment ago, and I suddenly remembered what Lynn had said about a broken engagement. After a moment he answered, "I asked first."

He was trying hard to keep the light tone, but it wasn't working too well. I debated whether to probe further, and decided it wasn't a good idea. Not now, anyway.

"Not much to tell," I told him. "I was so busy working to put myself through college that I didn't have a lot of time for dating. I've only had one serious relationship." I paused, then decided to tell him all of it. "No, that's not quite the way it was. *I* thought it was serious. Bruce felt otherwise."

"So that's why you've been so cagey with me?"

I started collecting the remains of our picnic, already sorry that I'd mentioned Bruce. "I haven't been any more cagey than you have," I said. I folded the tablecloth and removed the hamper from the blanket.

"You've got a point."

He sounded so much closer that I glanced up and was startled to find him only inches away, looking at me with an expression that made my breath catch in my throat.

"Dana," he sighed, curving his big, warm hand around my cheek. "You're quite a woman. I really do" — he hesitated — "like you a lot."

I swallowed. What was he about to say before he changed his mind? Never mind. If I had any sense, I'd get up and move away. But I didn't. Instead, I waited for what I was sure was coming next. And I was right. Jordan lowered his head and his lips touched mine, tentatively at first, but then, as I responded, his kiss grew deeper.

When we finally broke apart, I was breathless and a little shaky — Bruce's kisses had never affected me like this. I swallowed and then scrambled to my feet. "It's getting late. I guess we should get back." My voice must have sounded as breathless as I felt.

Jordan looked at me for a moment, his face very serious. Then he nodded. "Yes, I guess we'd better."

He got up too, and picked up the hamper. We walked in silence back to the car. Then, as I stood there and drank in the beauty all around me, he walked to my side and looked out over the valley with me.

"It's the most beautiful place I've ever seen," I told him, wishing he'd put his arm around me and draw me close.

He didn't, but he placed his hand lightly on my shoulder. "I think so too. I have from the first moment I saw it." He paused, then went on: "Do you think you could be happy living somewhere like this, so far out in the country?"

I felt myself stiffen. What did he mean by that? I couldn't tell from his expression, which didn't have the intentness of a few minutes ago. So I'd better play it cautious too. "I'm not sure," I said. "I've never really thought about it." That wasn't the exact truth. I could live here very happily, if Jordan asked me to.

"It's pretty isolated." His hand dropped from my shoulder. "I wanted to show you the inside of the house, but we can do that some other time." His voice sounded only friendly now.

"Yes, I'd like that," I answered. Disappointment swept over me, and not only because I would have liked to see the inside of the house. But I was relieved that I hadn't tried to make more out of what he'd asked than he'd intended. And that I hadn't been foolish enough to think that one kiss would make him want to propose to me.

When we got into the car, the sun was beginning to set and the evening breezes were rising. "Do you want the top up?" Jordan asked.

"No, this will be fine," I told him.

We drove back to Cedar Grove, neither of us saying much. The cool air blew over us, and I finally had to pull back my hair with a rubber band.

Jordan carried the hamper into the hallway, where we were greeted by a frantic Smoke. I'd never left him alone this long before, and he let me know in no uncertain terms that he didn't like it a bit, and that, as usual, he was starving.

"All right, all right, I'll get your dinner."

As I glanced at Jordan, who'd stooped to rub his hand down Smoke's arching back, my mouth curved in a smile. Cats knew the people who liked them, all right.

"Would you like to have some coffee before you go?" I asked.

Jordan straightened up and shook his head. "No, thanks. I'd better be getting home."

He stood there for a moment, and I wondered if he was trying to decide whether to kiss me good night. That would be very nice. I wouldn't mind that at all.

But he gave me only a warm smile. "Good night, Dana. I'll see you in the morning."

"You will?" I asked, because we had nothing scheduled. In fact, I'd purposely not told him about any more problems with the house, because he'd already done too much.

"Yes, I'm going to exercise the horses while it's still cool. How would you like to ride Sally?"

The question took me by surprise — I hadn't ridden Sally since the day we'd brought the horses over. I'd thought about asking him if he wanted me to exercise as well as feed and water them when he was gone, but I hadn't.

"I'd love to. What time?"

"About seven. That all right with you?"

"Fine." I hesitated, then asked him, "Want to have breakfast here? Just cereal and fruit — but you *do* like my coffee."

"All right. That sounds good," he answered, smiling.

I smiled back, then walked to the door with him. A few moments later I heard the sound of the Thunderbird leaving.

"I really *am* going to feed you — right now," I told Smoke. I'd eaten so much at our picnic that I knew I wouldn't be hungry until tomorrow. It was just as well I didn't have to cook any dinner, because I had a full evening ahead of me.

You're getting compulsive about this, I told myself as I headed for my office. Maybe so, but I couldn't let a day go by now without working on my story. Or was it Aunt Edith's story? The real and the make-believe were so blended now that there was no way to separate them — nor did I want to.

My life suddenly seemed very good. I liked living in this house in this small town. I had enough money to get by. And writing was satisfying some deep need I hadn't even known I had.

Best of all, I was beginning to hope that Jordan and I might have a future together. We'd gotten to know each other a lot better, and our kiss in the orchard had seemed to promise more to come.

The cautious part of me warned that maybe things were going too fast, but I ignored it. I wasn't rushing into anything and neither was Jordan. We were both still a little wary, but that was changing.

I picked up Smoke and cuddled him. "Things are looking up for us, do you know that?" When he squirmed and protested, I let him down and took the cover off the typewriter.

One bad relationship doesn't mean that you can't have a good one, I thought cheerfully, and then sat down to immerse myself in the past.

Chapter Seven

Smoke was tapping my face at six o'clock the next morning, but I was already awake and looking forward to the new day. My writing session the night before had gone well, but it had had a side effect I was becoming used to — I'd stayed awake for a long time, my mind whirling with the characters in my book.

"So by all rights I should be tired and grouchy," I told Smoke as I quickly dressed in jeans and a green T-shirt and went downstairs. But, surprisingly, I wasn't. And I knew why too — because I was going to spend the morning with Jordan. *If you're smart, you won't let him become that important in your life until you're sure how you feel about him — and how he really feels about you,* my ever-watchful mind monitor prodded me, but I ignored it again, as I was getting quite expert at doing.

I'd told Jordan to expect only fruit and cereal, but I found a package of muffin mix and thought, *Why not?* When he knocked on the door, promptly at seven, a tantalizing aroma filled the downstairs.

He sniffed. "What smells so good?" he asked, stepping inside. He wore well-worn, faded jeans too, and an equally old navy blue T-shirt. I felt a small tremor go through me as I remembered yesterday's kiss.

"Blueberry muffins," I said as he followed me to the kitchen. "It's a mix," I added as his face lit up.

"If they taste as good as they smell, who cares?"

I poured him a mug of coffee, and in a minute we were sitting across from each other with our muffins and orange juice and cereal.

He looked around the kitchen. "What have you done to this room? It looks brighter, more cheerful."

Just a couple of days ago I'd put up yellow curtains from my L.A. apartment, replacing the faded and flowered ones. I'd also made yellow covers for the chair cushions from some material I had, and I had placed a couple of inexpensive braided rugs on the old linoleum.

"You mean you sew?" he asked, sounding surprised. "I thought that was just about a lost art."

"I learned a long time ago, when money was tight in college."

He tilted his head and gave me an appraising look, as if seeing me in a new light.

"I had no idea you were so talented."

I laughed. "I'd hardly call sewing and making-do with what you have a talent."

"No, it's more than that. Some people have a knack for this sort of thing — and you're one of them."

I couldn't understand why he was making such a big deal out of what I'd done, but it warmed me inside, even while it made me a little uncomfortable for some reason I didn't quite understand. I buttered a muffin and didn't answer him.

"These are really good," Jordan said as he followed suit.

"Mixes are improving all the time. You should try them sometime."

"I'm not much of a cook. My house-keeper leaves me a meal the three days a week she comes in."

Now it was my turn to be surprised, although I shouldn't have been. "Oh, so you have a housekeeper? What does she do when you're in the remodeling stage on a house?"

"We haven't worked that out yet. Mrs. Robbins came to work for me right after I bought this last house." He smiled at me again and our glances met. Then his smile slowly faded.

I was holding my coffee mug halfway to

my mouth, and my hand froze at the look I thought I saw in his eyes. The look seemed to tell me he remembered that kiss yesterday just as vividly as I did.

I snapped myself out of my trance and hurriedly finished my coffee. Suddenly, this scene seemed a little too intimate, and I wanted to get out in the fields with the horses.

Jordan must have felt the same way, because he pushed back his chair at once. "Guess we should be getting outside while it's still cool. It's supposed to be a hot day."

With only a little help from Jordan, I saddled and bridled Sally while he took care of Ranger. Soon we were riding down the field into the lower pastures.

I took deep breaths of the fresh morning air, glad to be alive, to be exactly where I was, and to be doing just what I was doing. I glanced over at Jordan and found him looking at me.

"Isn't it a wonderful morning?" I asked. "We should do this every day." *I shouldn't have said that,* I told myself at once, because he would now think I was fishing for him to ask me to go riding every day.

But he didn't seem to. Instead, he gave me a quick glance and said, "I'd like nothing better, but, unfortunately, I'll have to be in Virginia at least two or three days a week for the next few months." He paused, then asked, "Would you like to exercise the horses when I'm not here? That is, if you have the time?"

I wanted to tell him that I'd rather ride *with* him than in place of him, but of course I didn't. "I'd be glad to, Jordan," I said instead. I would find the time; I owed him and would also enjoy it. "I need the exercise too, and this is more fun than bike riding."

He gave me a quick glance. "So you like to bike? I should have known. After all, you're one of those golden California girls, aren't you?"

His words didn't put me on the defensive, because for the first time he sounded as if he were genuinely teasing. There were no barbed undertones in his voice. So I answered in kind. "Not *very* golden. In case you hadn't noticed, I'm a redhead."

"Oh, I've noticed, all right," he answered, and his voice had lost its teasing intonation. "Your hair is like a flame and your eyes like the Pacific on a stormy day."

"Jordan, you have a way of coming out with the most surprising remarks," I said, trying to keep my voice light. I pushed my booted feet against Sally's sides, urging her to a faster gait.

"What's your hurry?" Jordan asked, catching up with me. "Do compliments always make you run away?"

"No. I just never know how to take you." We'd reached the fence marking the end of my land, and we turned our horses for the return trip.

"Why not just take me at face value," he said. "Whatever I say, I mean."

"What a novel, refreshing idea. Most people hide their true feelings much of the time."

"Yes, and that causes a lot of problems. I like people to know where I stand, and I expect the same from them." His voice had tightened a little.

Determined to keep this conversation on a bantering level, I asked, "Are you saying there's no place for the little white lie?"

He didn't turn toward me, and I saw that his profile had hardened too. "There's not much of a dividing line between a white lie and the real thing."

"I disagree," I said, hearing my voice come out crisper than I'd intended. But his sudden mood swings were wearing on the nerves, and, besides, I thought him dead wrong on this subject. "I don't think people could stand each other at close quarters for very long if everyone always told the absolute truth."

"I guess that's the way a lot of women feel. But I was beginning to think maybe you were different."

That hurt, and I threw him a tight-lipped glance. "Do you think I'm a liar, Jordan?" I demanded. "If so, I'd like to know what you base that idea on." I drew Sally to a stop and turned toward him. "Or are you just trying to pick a fight with me?"

He stopped too, and his eyes burned into mine for a moment. Then his face relaxed and he shook his head. "No, of course I don't. And I'm not trying to pick a fight. I'm sorry. I didn't mean to sound off like that."

I took a deep breath and then let it out, my anger fading away. He'd been so prompt and forthright with his apology that I had to accept it. I wanted to, anyway. "Good," I said. "Because I don't want to fight. I was having a glorious ride."

He answered my smile with one of his own. "So was I. Let's just forget my big mouth and enjoy the morning."

So we did. For the next half hour we rode and talked casually about a dozen different things: the house at the north end of town he'd just bought and was going to start restoring soon; his nieces and nephew; my plans to substitute-teach until the permanent position opened up at the end of the year; going to the band concert next Saturday."

I carefully kept the conversation away from all the things that still needed to be done to my house. Thanks to Jordan, I now had a sound roof over my head, and hot water, and a solid chimney that would allow me to build fires in the fireplaces come winter.

He turned down my offer of more coffee, and as he opened the back gate to leave, he bent his head and kissed me. "I enjoyed our ride, Dana. See you in the morning?"

His kiss had been quick, but not too fast for me to respond. I nodded and answered "yes," wishing he would kiss me again.

He didn't, though. I watched him stride down the country road toward his house, my heart still beating faster than normal and my knees a little shaky.

Inside, I poured myself another mug of coffee and sat at the table to drink it. Smoke ambled over and gave me one of his inquiring sounds. "Come on," I told him, patting my lap. He leaped up and settled down, purring.

I envied him his easy contentment. Jordan didn't make me feel contented. No, he stirred me up, made me feel alive and eager, made me want more of his kisses and caresses all the time. He also puzzled and irritated me sometimes — but so what? I wasn't perfect, either, and there were no perfect relationships. *I* should know that.

Besides, I somehow had the feeling that Jordan's sudden attacks of moodiness weren't really indicative of his true personality.

No, something was bothering him, something he didn't want to talk about. I wished I could think of a way to get it out of him.

I knew that Jordan was attracted to me and had some kind of feelings for me. But there was something not quite right between us. And even though he'd apologized for upsetting me during our ride, I was sure he meant every word of what he'd said about hating subterfuge.

I also felt sure that that had something to do with whatever was wrong between us. I wished I knew what it was. Because I'd just become aware of something else. All my warnings to myself to take it slow and easy, to be cautious and wary this time, hadn't worked. I was falling in love with Jordan.

"Blythe, do you know anything about stripping wallpaper?" I asked. It was Thursday, two days after Jordan and I had first ridden together and we'd been out both mornings. He'd kissed me good-bye each day, and sometimes the kisses weren't so casual, but our conversations during the rides hadn't enlightened me at all as to how he really felt. Now he was off to Virginia again for a couple of days.

Blythe looked around my kitchen, where we were having coffee and the apple dumplings she'd brought over. She shook her head and said, "Wallpaper wasn't my department. Harold always did those things or we hired somebody. This paper is in pretty bad shape."

I sighed. "Yes, and so are all the other rooms. But I'm with you, I've never done anything like that. And when I tried pulling off a little piece, it took half the plaster too."

"I thought Jordan was helping you fix the place up," Blythe remarked, giving me a sort of arch look. "He's been over here a lot."

"He's done too much already — a lot more than he should have in exchange for boarding his horses here. And right now I can't afford to pay anyone else."

Trying to keep my expression casual, I took a bite of dumpling covered with warm lemon-nutmeg sauce. I closed my eyes and sighed in appreciation. "Blythe, you're the best cook in the world. And speaking of people being places — what about you and Thomas Parker?"

Blythe blushed and turned her attention to her own dumpling. "Oh, he's just a friend. Why is it when a woman has a man friend, everyone just automatically assumes there's something romantic involved?"

Glad to be off the hook myself, I grinned as I said, "Because there usually is and you know it." I realized my mistake too late.

"Then that means you and Jordan are more than just friends too?" she asked, a gleam in her eyes.

I started to shake my head, then decided not to deny it. *What? No little white lie?* my inner guide asked. *Are you beginning to think like Jordan?* I wasn't sure about that, but I knew Blythe was no gossip. "Blythe, what would you do if you thought you were falling in love with a man and you weren't sure how he felt about you? And you also had a feeling that something was wrong between you, and you didn't know what it was?"

She gave me a long, level look, then shook her head. "I don't know, Dana," she said after some thought. "Maybe you could just come right out and ask him?"

"That thought has occurred to me," I told

her. Yes, especially after Jordan's little speech about honesty. "I consider myself as liberated as the next woman, but somehow I just can't bring myself to tell Jordan I think I'm falling in love with him and I'd like to know what his own feelings are."

"Liberated or not, we usually leave it to the man to speak first, don't we?"

I gave her a wry smile. "How true. And Jordan and I haven't known each other very long."

"It doesn't take long to know these things," Blythe said. "Why, even that first night at the band concert, I knew I wanted to see Thomas again." She gave me a sly smile. "Well, you were honest with me, so I guess I owe you the same."

"I'm glad for you, Blythe. Thomas is a nice man."

"Yes, he is. I think he's getting serious, and I'm not doing a thing to discourage him. That old house has been mighty lonesome since Harold passed away. It would be nice to have someone else there with me."

"Just anyone?" I teased her.

She shook her head. "Nope, not just anyone. I never thought I'd look at another man, but Thomas and I like the same kind of life, and already he's gotten involved with community things. He's the new chairman of the Council on Senior Services and Activities." She beamed proudly.

As we said good-bye a few minutes later, I envied her even as I wished her well and hoped she'd find happiness and companionship. If only my relationship with Jordan were that simple, and I had more money, and more typing jobs, and I'd get the teaching position in December.

And if only I hadn't hit a snag in my book. For two days now I hadn't been able to write anything I liked, and my wastebasket was full of discarded pages. I was tired of the whole thing and hated everything about it, but something inside me wouldn't let me quit.

And you have a strip of wall with the plaster falling off and you've got to figure out something to do with it, I told myself. *So it's back to the library for those how-to books.*

"Well, how's your love life?" Lynn asked me as we sat on our lawn chairs on Saturday night, listening to the band.

"Don't ask," I told her. "I'm learning how to patch plaster and strip wallpaper, and that's enough for me to deal with right now."

"That would be more than enough for me," she commented. "Can't you just paint

127

over it or something?"

"No, it's too far gone. I guess I could be doing worse. I found some rolls of wallpaper in the attic, and I've ruined only about half of them so far." My tone was light, but I wasn't exaggerating.

"Seriously, though, Dana, what's with you and Jordan? I know you see each other a lot. Don't try to tell me that neither one of you is romantically interested in the other."

"Truthfully, I don't know what's going on with us." I took a deep breath and decided that since I'd told Blythe how I felt about Jordan, I might as well tell Lynn too. She was no blabbermouth, either. "I think I'm falling in love with him, but he hasn't said anything to me about love."

I half expected her to advise me to ask him, but she didn't. She sighed and shook her head. "Problems, problems. You want to settle down here with Jordan and live cozily ever after, and I want to get away from here so bad I can't think straight."

"Well, then, why don't you?" I asked, glad to have the subject changed. "You can move away if you want to. Though I'd miss you." That was very true. We'd become good friends in a short time.

"It's not that simple," she said, frowning. "I've never been more than two hundred miles from Cedar Grove. I don't know where I want to go, I don't have much money saved, and I have a good job I'd be foolish to give up."

"Couldn't you get a transfer to a different post office?"

"Maybe, but jobs are tight right now. Most people are staying put and not many are quitting or retiring."

"Maybe I could write to some people I know in L.A. Not about a post office job, but other kinds. Think you'd like working as a bank teller?"

Lynn's eyes lit up. "Could you really?" Then she frowned. "I don't know. Maybe I'm crazy, but I'll think over the idea of a different job. I'm too young to worry about job security."

"I can't argue with you about that, since I quit a good job in L.A. to come here," I told her. Yes, and maybe I'd been a fool too. My savings were going faster than I'd planned, and the only typing work I could count on was the stuff I did a couple of times a week for Mr. Hadley.

Just then, I glanced over at Jordan and saw he was looking at me. He gave me a special little smile that warmed me through and through. I smiled back, trying to make it special for him too. Maybe both of us were sort of treading water with each other, but I suddenly felt better about the situation.

That's probably because you've told Lynn and Blythe you love Jordan, my sensible half informed me. *As if that will help matters any. You haven't told Jordan and you don't know how he feels about you, and that's what counts.*

Chapter Eight

"You've painted the kitchen," Jordan said, glancing around at the new off-white walls. We'd just finished our early-morning riding session and he'd come in for coffee.

"Yes, I did it yesterday. I decided it wouldn't be a good idea to put up unwashable wallpaper in here, and that's all I had."

Since my story was still bogged down, I'd decided to take a few days off. And although I didn't mention it to Jordan, I hadn't finished the job until nearly midnight. After pricing vinyl wallpapers, I'd quickly opted for paint even if it didn't look as good.

"The salesman steered me to some textured stuff," I said. "It covers the old wallpaper pretty well." I'd squeezed the price of two gallons out of my latest work for Mr. Hadley. I'd also picked up a couple of college midterm papers to bring a little more money in, thank goodness.

Jordan poured mugs of coffee for us, and then he smiled at me. "Yes, it does cover the old paper. You're getting very resourceful. So you've been doing some wallpapering too? Where?"

"My bedroom and the living room." After much trial and error those two rooms were looking pretty good, and I was proud of myself. Maybe I couldn't drive nails straight, but I could paint and hang wallpaper.

"I'd like to see." He took his coffee and headed toward the living room.

I had no choice but to follow, feeling a little nervous about his reaction. After all, he was a professional and I was merely an amateur.

The wallpaper was a small-patterned, old-fashioned print in shades of greens and browns. It went well with the room and its bow window and window seat, twins to the ones upstairs in my bedroom.

Jordan's glance took in the moss-green throws I'd brought with me from my apartment in L.A. and put on the old sofa and chair. I'd also found some fabric remnants on sale at Cedar Grove's only discount store. I'd sewn brown-and-green striped covers for the window seat and maple rocker cushions, with enough left over for swags at the windows. A braided rug from one of the bedrooms was now on the newly waxed floor.

He turned back to me, a surprised and approving look in his eyes. "You've done a great job in here!"

I felt a warm glow because I was sure his approval was genuine. Not only had Jordan told me he always said what he thought, but I didn't think he could fake this kind of thing, even if he wanted to.

"Thanks. Wallpapering really isn't that hard once you get the hang of it." *And God should strike you dead for lying,* I told myself, remembering the struggles I'd had at first.

"It's hard enough. But I was talking about the whole room. You've made it warm and inviting, just as you did the kitchen. You have a real talent for that. Better than a lot of professional decorators."

I felt a little embarrassed by his praise. "Oh, come on now, that's going too far."

He shook his head. "No, it's not. I mean every word of it." He paused, then went on. "I'd like to talk to you about something while we finish our coffee."

Mystified, I nodded. "Of course." We went back to the kitchen and sat down again. I took a sip of coffee, then smiled at him. "All right, shoot."

He smiled back, then asked, "How would you like to work with me on the next house I restore?"

I blinked. "This is really a surprise."

"I like what you've done here, as I said. I think we could work well together."

"I appreciate your offer, Jordan, but school starts in just a few weeks." And between now and then, I wanted to get my book finished. But I wasn't going to tell him about that. I still wasn't sure where I was going with it.

He lifted an eyebrow. "You'll only be substituting. You don't know if you'll get the permanent position or not, right?"

I shrugged, feeling uncomfortable at his insistence. "That's true, but I do know I'd much rather teach than work on houses." I gave him a smile to take the sting out of my refusal.

"All right. It was just an idea."

I still felt uncomfortable, because his voice sounded a little stiff. "I'm sorry, Jordan," I said. "It's a great offer, and if. . . ."

He smiled at me. "Don't worry about it. I can see your point. After all, teaching is a profession you've worked hard for. I couldn't expect you to give it up." He got to his feet. "I have to go, but there's something else I want to talk to you about before I leave."

"Sure. Go ahead."

"I'm going to visit my family this Sunday. Would you like to come along and meet them?"

"You're just full of surprises this morning," I told him as a tiny flutter of nervousness hit my stomach. "Yes, I'd like that."

He smiled back. "Good. I plan to leave in the morning, at about nine. Mom still fixes a big Sunday dinner for the clan."

I swallowed. So he meant not just his parents but all his family. "That sounds fine," I managed to say. "Uh, how shall I dress?"

"Oh, just a skirt and blouse or something like that. Slacks, if you want to. My family isn't at all formal."

"Fine. I'll be ready."

Jordan pushed his chair back and got up. "Well, since the band isn't having a concert this week, I guess I won't see you until then. Tomorrow morning, I have to go to Virginia again, and I won't be back until Saturday evening."

I walked him to the door, and he gave me a warmer-than-usual good-bye kiss. Warmer and longer. I could still feel his taste on my lips long after he'd closed the door behind him. I found myself humming as I washed our mugs and headed for the office. Smoke was asleep in my desk chair, and he stalked off indignantly when I routed him out.

I turned on the typewriter and rolled in a sheet of paper, feeling a mixture of anticipation and nervousness. I couldn't help but feel that Jordan's asking me to meet his family meant he was ready for our relationship to progress — and so was I.

But in the midst of my happy thoughts, something kept nagging at me. I couldn't get rid of my idea that Jordan had been more upset about my refusal to work with him than he'd let on. He'd tried hard not to show his feelings — and had almost succeeded.

There was still some kind of barrier between us, and I still didn't know what it was. Maybe it had something to do with his parents. Maybe I would find out this weekend. I hoped so.

"How long is it since you visited Philly?" Jordan asked me as we approached the city. He was driving the Thunderbird again, but with the top up this time.

I thought for a minute, glad to put my mind on something other than the meeting with his family. "About a year before we moved to California, I guess," I finally answered. "Thirteen or fourteen years ago. Of course, we did all the usual tourist things — saw Independence Hall, the Liberty Bell, the art museum."

"I'm always amazed at how many firsts there are here," Jordan said. "The Walnut

Street Theater is the oldest active theater in the country, and the Academy of Natural Sciences is also the oldest institution of its kind."

"I'd forgotten all that, but it's coming back to me. Sometime I'd like to spend a weekend seeing everything again."

"I'd like to take you."

His prompt offer gave me a warm glow, calming the butterflies that were now attacking in droves. "I'd like to go." I gave him a quick smile.

He smiled back, then reached for my hand. "Your hand is cold. What's wrong?"

"I'm pretty nervous about meeting your family."

His hand tightened on mine, sending a thrill of pleasure up my arm. "What in the world for? They're very ordinary people. And you look fine. You'll bowl them over."

I glanced down at my jade-green shirt-waist dress and white low-heeled pumps, hoping he was right. I didn't think I would bowl them over, but I wanted them to like me at least.

Jordan put on his turn signal and took an exit that put us on the bypass around the city. "Doesn't your family live in the city?" I asked.

"They live in the suburbs, in the same

house where we all grew up. Mom says they'll have to carry her out feet-first to get her to move."

I relaxed a little more at this information, realizing I'd subconsciously been expecting him to take me to one of the restored town houses on Society Hill or somewhere like that.

Half an hour later he pulled up before a white, two-story house with brown shutters and trim in a nice neighborhood of spacious lots and big shade trees. The house was set back from the street with a large front lawn. Several cars were parked in the driveway.

"Here we are," he announced. "Looks like everyone is already here."

I got out, my nervousness back full force, and wishing we'd gotten here earlier, so that I wouldn't have to face the assembled family.

We went up the walk and Jordan rang the doorbell. I heard footsteps, and then the door swung open. A tall woman, who had to be Jordan's mother, stood there, smiling broadly at us. "Jordan! It's so good to see you. You don't come home often enough." She hugged him, then turned to me.

She had graying dark hair and Jordan's dark eyes, and was dressed in navy slacks and a white blouse. "And you must be

Dana." She gave me a welcoming smile, then hugged me too. "We're so glad you could come."

I hugged her back, relieved at the warm welcome. "I'm glad to meet you, Mrs. Meade," I answered, smiling back.

"Call me Anita," she said. "Come on along to the family room and meet the family." She led the way down the wide front hall and then took a door to the left.

The room was filled with people, all talking at once and with the television going too. In a minute, I sorted them out and saw there were three men including a middle-aged man who was obviously Jordan's father — and two women, who must be his brothers' wives. There were also three children, ranging from four or so up to eight or nine. A long-haired white cat was curled in a chair, and I remembered Jordan's saying that his mother always had at least one cat.

Everyone gave us warm smiles as we entered, and after Anita performed the introductions, I realized that my tension had melted in the warmth of their friendliness. I liked his brothers, Scott and Phil, at once, and also their wives. His father was friendly too, but in a gruff, no-nonsense way.

"Dinner, everyone," Anita called.

Jordan and I joined the procession into a

large, cheerful dining room, its long table filled with bowls and platters. Anita waved me to a place beside Jordan, and when we were all seated, she passed me a platter of pot roast. "We don't eat like this all the time," she said after I'd helped myself. Next she urged a bowl of mashed potatoes on me. "Now that everyone's watching their weight, we do this only on special occasions."

"Yes, young lady, I'm certainly glad you're here," Jordan's father, Lawton, said, ladling gravy all over his mashed potatoes. "Only time I get real food anymore is when we have company."

I felt a mixture of emotions at the thought that I was "special company," but I smiled back and said, "Everything looks so good."

"Jordan tells us your family lived in Cedar Grove years ago," Anita said after everyone was served. "And you decided to move back?"

"Yes. I realized how much I'd missed it. And I really like small-town living."

"I wouldn't want to be that far away from Philly. We've lived here so long."

"Never could understand why Jordan moved there," his father said. His bushy gray brows drew together in a frown as he glanced at his youngest son. "We need him in the business."

I felt Jordan tense beside me, and realized this must be an old argument.

"No, you don't, Dad," he said in a moment. His voice was even, but I could tell it was an effort for him to keep it that way. "You and Scott and Phil do just fine."

"I built this business from the ground up for you boys to take over," his father continued, his face reddening a little. "That was all I ever wanted."

"Lawton, please." Anita's voice was crisp. "Let's not get into all that again."

Lawton looked mutinously at her for a moment. Then he pressed his lips together and turned to his plate.

Phil said something quickly, Anita answered, and the awkward moment was smoothed over. But Jordan remained full of tension as the meal continued.

He must go through this every time he comes home for a visit, I thought. Which probably explained his mother's statement that he didn't come home often enough.

Fudge cake ended the meal, and by the time I finished my huge slice, I felt as if I'd never be able to eat again. "Dana's going to help me with the dishes," Anita announced as everyone got up from the table. "I want to get to know her."

No one objected to that plan, and the adults dispersed to the family room and the children went outside. Jordan threw me an inquiring glance over his shoulder as he left, and I smiled back to let him know that this was all right with me. He still had tension lines around his mouth, I saw.

"So, tell me all about yourself, Dana," Anita said as we loaded the dishwasher. "Jordan's so close-mouthed we didn't know anything about you until he called to say he was bringing you today."

That information made me a little uncomfortable. "There's not too much to tell," I said, and then explained the circumstances that had brought me back to Cedar Grove.

"So you're all alone in the world?" Anita asked, her voice full of sympathy.

"Afraid so," I said lightly.

She laid her hand on my shoulder, comfortingly. "That's terrible! Everyone needs a family." Then she smiled a little ruefully. "I know you must think that this one doesn't get along very well, but we really do. Only one thing gets Lawton going, and you were a witness to that a few minutes ago."

I returned her smile, not quite knowing how to answer. In a moment I said, "Jordan is a very independent person."

She nodded vigorously as she wiped off the countertop. "He's just like his father, and that's why they clash. Lawton may have built up the business for his sons, but he still wants to run things!"

As our glances met, we smiled again and I felt very close to her. It was an odd feeling, as if I'd known her a long time, and I liked it. "I don't think Jordan would let anyone run his life," I finally commented.

She laughed. "You've got it! It's just as well he left to make it on his own, but we miss him. If his father would accept that Jordan isn't coming back to the company and leave him alone, I think Jordan would visit more often."

"He probably would," I agreed. I felt that I'd been given some of the missing pieces to what made Jordan tick, but not all of them.

"Dana, I'm really glad that Jordan is . . . interested in you. You're the first woman he's dated since Vanessa broke their engagement," Anita said.

The moments ticked by as I digested this information. So, Lynn had been right, although she didn't know Jordan hadn't been dating. Finally I glanced over at his mother and forced a smile. "We really haven't talked about any of that, Mrs. Meade."

"Call me Anita," she said again, her eyes searching mine and her face a little troubled. "I hope I haven't said anything to upset you, but I just assumed Jordan would have told you."

"Don't worry about it," I assured her.

She touched my shoulder again. "Believe me, none of us were sorry when that engagement was broken."

I didn't know how to answer that, so I said nothing. From then on, the talk was casual, and after finishing the dishes, we joined the others in the family room.

When Jordan shot me a glance, I gave him a wide smile. His father was watching television, but something in his stiff back and in Jordan's tense jawline made me think that they had argued again.

Sensing that the atmosphere needed to be lightened up, Anita brought out several photograph albums and showed me Jordan as a baby and toddler and then up through his high-school graduation picture.

I picked up an album and leafed through it idly, but I paused for a long, close look when I came to a page where Jordan was standing next to a stunning black-haired woman. She was smiling into the camera with a very self-assured expression, and she and Jordan were holding hands.

I stared at the photo, then glanced up to find Anita's eyes on it too. She gave me a tiny nod, and I knew she meant that the woman in the photo was Vanessa. I snapped the album closed and put it back on the table, feeling a knot forming in my stomach.

No wonder that Jordan had had the props knocked out from under him when she broke their engagement; Vanessa was one of the most beautiful women I'd ever seen.

Jordan had been talking with his brothers, and just then he turned back to me. "It's about time we left," he said a little abruptly. "I have to go to Virginia in the morning."

Since he'd just gotten back from there last night, that surprised me, but I nodded. "Yes, I guess we'd better go."

Jordan's father left the TV to say good-bye to us, but he and Jordan were still stiff with each other, I noticed. Anita hugged me again, and I hugged her back with genuine affection. I liked her, as well as the rest of Jordan's family.

Jordan let out a sigh of relief as he pulled onto the street. "I'm sorry about all that," he told me.

I glanced over at him. A muscle was clenched in his jaw.

"Don't worry about it," I said, making my

voice light. "All families have these little disagreements." The minute I'd said it, I wished I hadn't. I'd made *too* light of it, I knew.

Jordan let out a snort of mirthless laughter. "*Little* disagreements? Dad and I can't even have a civil conversation since I walked out on the family business." He banged a fist on the steering wheel.

I reached over and touched his arm. The muscles felt bunched and tight under my hand. "Don't you think that if you give him time, your father will accept your choice?"

"How much time would you suggest? Six years seems plenty long enough to me."

I bit my lip, trying to think of some way to defuse his anger and resentment. "I don't know what to tell you," I finally said. "Except that I'd trade your problems with your family for *my* situation. At least you *have* a family."

I heard him take a long breath and then let it out. Then he reached over and squeezed my hand. "Thanks, Dana," he said, his voice softer and less angry. "I needed to be reminded of that fact."

Warmth from his touch spread up my arm, and I relaxed too. "Think nothing of it," I said lightly. "Just my good deed for the day."

"I wish I didn't have to go back to Virginia tomorrow."

Was that a leading question? I wondered. After a moment I said, "Me too," and waited for something else.

But there was nothing else. As Jordan relapsed into brooding silence, I hoped that I had helped him some, but it would take more than a few words from me to straighten out his problems with his father.

"Do you want to come in for coffee?" I asked Jordan as we approached my house.

He shook his head, that withdrawn expression still on his face. "No, I'd better head on home. I have to get up at four in the morning."

I forced a smile. "Thanks for taking me today. I really enjoyed it."

"I'll see you when I get back," he said. He reached out and touched my cheek for a moment. Then he left without kissing me good-bye.

If I'd thought that this visit with his family was going to resolve anything between us, I'd certainly been wrong, I told myself as I went to the kitchen, trying to fend off a ravenous Smoke.

If anything, the visit had made things worse. And I wasn't at all sure that the recurring argument with his father was the only thing that was bothering him. Maybe the return to Philadelphia had reminded him of Vanessa and had brought all that unhappiness back full force.

Maybe, I forced myself to admit, he had never gotten over the woman. Maybe I was just a substitute and he'd realized it today when he went back to the city where she lived. Maybe that was why he hadn't kissed me good-bye when he left.

And maybe, I told myself grimly as I spooned cat food into Smoke's dish, *you're going to get yourself into that office and sit there with your book until you figure out what went wrong with it. That should keep your busy little mind occupied for a while!*

Chapter Nine

I brought Lynn a glass of iced tea and put it on the end table next to her. She didn't look up from the stack of typewritten sheets on her lap. I stood there for a moment, then went back to the kitchen and tried to relax.

Lynn was reading my book, and I wasn't at all sure that I should have let her. What if she hated it? Would that depress me so much that I would never finish it? This had all come about because she'd dropped in unexpectedly one evening when I was working on the book and I was so preoccupied that she finally got it out of me.

"You're doing *what?*" she'd cried, her eyes wide with surprise.

So I'd told her the whole story about Aunt Edith's letters and her tragic romance. From there, it was just a short step to her begging me to let her read the manuscript.

That had been two hours ago. I took a deep breath and marched back to the office. "Lynn," I said, and when she didn't look up, I said it again, louder. "It's eleven o'clock. Maybe you'd better finish reading tomorrow."

She looked up, still holding on to the sheet of paper. "I'm almost finished," she said, and returned to reading.

I sighed and went back to the kitchen. Ten minutes later she appeared in the doorway with the pile of manuscript. She didn't say anything, just stood there holding it. I gave her a nervous look.

"Well, what do you think? Should I bum it?" I asked, only half jokingly. A few days ago I'd finally solved the problem that had had me stymied, but had immediately encountered others.

She shook her head and gave me a ferocious frown. "Don't you even think of such a thing! This is great! Why didn't you tell me you were doing this?" she demanded.

"I don't know. It just started out as something I had to do to keep the ideas running around in my head from driving me crazy, and it sort of snowballed from there." I glanced at her skeptically. "You really think this is good? You're not just saying that because we're friends?"

She shook her head again, harder, and plopped down beside me on a kitchen chair. "Of course not. This is really good. I couldn't put it down, and isn't that supposed to be the acid test?"

"Don't ask *me*," I said as emotions welled

up inside me: elation and hope; the fear that she was wrong, that *I* was wrong and the book was garbage. "I can't figure out how to end it. I can't stand to kill off my hero and end it as unhappily as it was in real life."

Lynn looked horrified at that idea. "No, of course you can't do that! That would be terrible! Give it a happy ending."

"But then it's not really Aunt Edith's story," I told her. I felt mixed up and out of sorts, and all of it wasn't caused by my problems with the book. Jordan was still in Virginia, I presumed. At least, if he was back, he hadn't let me know. I'd been riding both horses each day, which I enjoyed, but I'd have enjoyed it a lot more if he'd been with me. I'd taken up a lot of time with it.

But then, I hadn't had any new typing clients, and I didn't have any more money to spend on the house, so it didn't really matter. I still had my afternoons and evenings for writing.

"So?" Lynn asked me, answering my question with one of her own. "What difference does that make? If you're going to get it published, you'll have to add a lot of made-up stuff."

"Get it published? What are you talking about? I never had any plans to do that." Maybe I had, I realized, but had been afraid to think along those lines.

"You've *got* to," Lynn insisted. "It's too good to stick in a desk drawer. Why, I bet you can get an agent interested in it. It could be a best-seller. Maybe you could even sell it to the movies."

I laughed out loud at her pipe dreams. "Yes, and any day now I'm going to win the lottery too. Come on, Lynn, get real."

She frowned at me and tapped her fingers on the pile of manuscript. "I'm not joking," she insisted. "How many books would ever get published if the writers didn't at least *try* to sell them?"

"None, I suppose. But this isn't even finished. I don't know if I can ever finish it to suit me."

She got up and deposited the stack of typed pages in my lap. "Of course you can," she said firmly. "If you've gotten this far, you can certainly finish it."

"Well, not tonight," I told her with finality, as I got up too. "I'm bushed. And you have to be up early too, don't you?"

"You know I do. The post office never rests except on Sundays and holidays, and tomorrow, unfortunately, is neither. I'll see you tomorrow evening."

"Why? I didn't know we had anything planned."

"We do now." She gave me a brilliant smile. "After work, I'm going to the library and see if I can find out anything about agents. That's what you need to sell a book these days — a good agent!"

"How do you know these things?" I asked her, genuinely surprised.

"I read magazines and newspapers," she said. "Every one of the best-selling authors has an agent."

"Now wait a minute," I protested, following her to the door. "You're going too fast. I haven't finished the book. And no agent would be interested in it, anyway."

"How do you know if you don't let them read it?"

With that very good question left hanging in the air, she made her exit.

"How have things been going?" Jordan asked me, making the turn onto the country road that led to his beautiful stone house. He was driving his pickup, its back filled with lumber and tools.

"Nothing of earth-shattering importance has happened," I told him. It was Sunday afternoon, a hot and muggy day late in July. Jordan had returned to town yesterday evening in time to play his saxophone in the concert. The four of us — Lynn, Cliff,

153

Jordan, and I — had gone to the inn again afterward.

We'd all had a good time, even though I'd had to kick Lynn under the table once or twice to keep her from telling Cliff and Jordan about my book.

True to her word, she'd ferreted out a list of agents and badgered me until I'd written a query letter to several of them. Now that the letters were in the mail, I wished I hadn't sent them. I'd probably never hear anything from the agents, and even if I did, they would hate the book.

"That's what I like about Cedar Grove," Jordan said, smiling at me. "I can get my excitement from the newspapers and TV."

"True." I returned his smile, glad he was back. I'd missed him a lot. I thought for a minute about telling him that, then decided against it. He hadn't told me he'd missed me, even though he had given me a lingering good-night kiss last night.

But his mood from last Sunday, after we returned from Philadelphia, was gone, and the tension produced by the visit to his family seemed to have worked itself out. Also, I'd decided I was crazy to think that he was still brooding over Vanessa. After all, that was in the past. I planned to enjoy today, not worry about Jordan's ex-fiancée.

I was going to see the inside of his house, and I was eagerly anticipating that. I didn't know why he had asked me to come today, but I was glad he had. As he turned onto the lane and drove down under the canopy of trees, I held my breath, waiting for the house to come into view.

When it did, it gave me the same thrill as before. "How did you ever find this place?" I asked as he pulled up before the house.

"I came over here to buy some apples from one of the orchards," he said, his expression the same as on that other day — pleasure and pride of ownership, "and saw the for-sale sign. I bought it that same day."

"I don't blame you. I would have too." We got out and walked to the front door side by side.

Close up, I could see that the house needed work. Chunks of mortar were missing from between the big gray fieldstones, and the windows and front door needed repairs and painting. Jordan searched in his pockets and found the key.

The door swung open into a spacious hallway with wide-planked pine flooring that was scuffed and stained. Wallpaper hung in strips from the ceiling, and clumps of plaster littered the floor. The doors stood open and I could see into rooms on both sides of the hall, and they were in the same state of disrepair. The staircase at the end of the hall was missing some banister posts. But none of that mattered; whoever built this house had known about design and structure, and its innate beauty showed through the grime and neglect.

I took a deep breath and let it out. "It's absolutely beautiful, Jordan," I told him. "I'd love to —" I stopped. I'd been about to say that I'd love to live here, but in view of the progress, or rather *lack* of progress of our relationship, I changed it to "see it when it's restored."

He gave me an odd look. "I hope you do too." Something in his voice didn't quite fit with what he'd said, and I wondered what it was.

For the next hour Jordan took me on a tour of the house, and I liked everything I saw, from the sunny, many-windowed kitchen to the big room upstairs that was going to be the master bedroom suite.

A smaller bedroom next to it would be converted into a bathroom. There were three other bedrooms upstairs, enough for at least three children. I shot a glance at Jordan, wondering what his thoughts were.

I was a little startled at his very intent look. "So you like the house, do you?" he asked, and again his voice had an odd note.

"Of course. How could anyone help liking it?"

He gave me a wry smile. "Oh, not everyone would, believe me. Some people would hate the thought of living way out here in this big old barn of a house."

"Well, I wouldn't. I'd love it." Maybe I'd said too much, but after all, he *had* asked me.

"That's not what you said the first time we were here," he reminded me.

I'd forgotten that he'd asked me the same thing the day of our picnic in the orchard, and I'd told him I wasn't sure.

"A lot has changed since then," I said in a moment, returning his look. Yes, the most momentous change being that I knew I loved him. A shiver whispered down my spine, giving me a spooky feeling. Something was going to happen in this dusty upstairs hallway, I was suddenly sure.

He stepped a little closer and reached for my hand. "What's changed, Dana?" he asked. "Your feelings for the house — or for me?"

As always, his hand enclosing mine made my heart beat faster. I swallowed at his directness, even though I should be used to it by now. Finally I nodded. "Yes, Jordan, to both questions."

"Do you care enough about me to live in this house with me?" he asked, his fingers squeezing my hand, his eyes still boring into mine with an intensity that made me want to step back from him.

"Are you asking me to marry you?" I asked, trying to keep my voice steady.

"Of course I'm asking you to marry me," he answered tenderly. "What did you think I meant?"

Joy bubbled up inside me. "You never know these days." I curved my free arm around his neck and smiled up at him. "Yes, I'll marry you, Jordan."

Relief filled his eyes, and he pulled me into his arms and kissed me long and deeply. When we finally drew apart, my knees were shaking.

"I was afraid last Sunday that my family might have scared you off," he said.

I smiled at him. "I won't be marrying your family." Jordan's kiss had been sweet and tender and had intensified my love for him. But something still nagged at me. Why hadn't he said that he loved me?

"No, you won't," he agreed. "We probably won't be seeing much of them unless my dad's attitude changes." He shook his head. "Enough of all that. I didn't get an engagement ring. I wasn't sure you'd accept me, and I also thought you might want to pick one out yourself."

I tried to shake off the feeling that something was wrong. He'd asked me to marry him, and so he must love me. Maybe he was just one of those men who found it hard to say the words. "Oh, so you weren't sure of me, were you?" I teased.

He reached out and brushed my hair back from my face. "No, I wasn't sure at all. Half the time you acted as skittish as a colt. I never knew how to take you."

"I could say the same thing about you," I told him, smiling.

He reached for my hand again, and stood there, idly running his fingers up my wrist. "Dana, I'd like us to marry soon. I see no reason to wait. Is that all right with you?"

I nodded, my mouth still curved in a smile. "Yes, it is."

He pulled me close and kissed me again. When the kiss was over, he traced the outline of my lips with one strong finger.

"I want to make this place into a home for us as soon as possible. I'd like us to start working on the house right away — together."

His words warmed me to my toes. There was nothing I'd rather do than work on this beautiful old house with the man I loved.

"That sounds great. I can't wait to start."

The minute I'd said the words, I remembered the book. How was I going to work on the house *and* finish it? Maybe I should tell Jordan about the book? *No,* I decided, *not now.* Not until I knew if one of the agents was interested.

I could do it — I'd write in the evenings, which I usually did, anyway. It would work out, I tried to reassure myself.

"I can't wait, either," Jordan answered. He kissed me again, lingeringly. Basking in the warm afterglow, I thought about how everything had turned out just the way I'd hoped. But a little nagging thought kept surfacing, no matter how I tried to ignore it: Why hadn't Jordan said he loved me? And another thought pushed in beside the first one: *Beware when things seem perfect.*

That was superstitious nonsense, and I wouldn't give it house room, I told myself impatiently. Nothing was going to happen to our relationship.

Jordan seemed to have finally gotten over his belief that I was a city person at heart and that my move to Cedar Grove was an impulsive whim that wouldn't last. Of course he had, or he wouldn't have asked me to marry him.

Everything was fine, wonderful, I repeated to myself. And I closed my ears to the little voice in my head that wouldn't shut up.

"Dana!" Lynn cried over the phone. "The first-class mail just came in, and there's a letter for you from another one of the agents you wrote to — Marla Williams."

"Which will no doubt say the same as the other three," I told her. " 'Sorry, but I don't feel sufficiently enthusiastic about this project to want to read it.' " I joked to steel myself against another disappointment.

Two weeks had passed since that day in Jordan's house. We'd spent a lot of time making plans about marriage and work on the house. We'd also gone to a jewelry store and picked out an engagement ring — a diamond flanked by rubies. It was beautiful and I loved it, though Jordan had wanted me to select a more expensive one.

It had been fun and exciting, even though I couldn't seem to get rid of that little niggling feeling of something not quite right. Jordan was now away in Virginia for a couple of days, but he was due back tomorrow.

"Don't be such a pessimist," Lynn scolded me. "I can't stand the suspense. If you don't hurry up and get on down here,

I'm going to open it myself."

"Go ahead. Read it to me."

I heard a ripping sound and then paper crackling, and pictured Lynn's impatient hands tearing at the envelope and taking the letter out.

Then I heard a sharp intake of breath and felt my heart skip a beat. Was it good news or bad?

"Dana! She likes the idea and wants to read the book! Isn't that great?"

I was too surprised to answer. After the three turndowns, I'd lost confidence that the book was any good.

"Dana — what's wrong? Did you faint?"

"No, of course not," I answered finally. "I'm just surprised, that's all."

"Well, *I'm* not," she said exuberantly. "I told you it was a good book. She wants to see it as soon as it's finished. You *are* working on it, aren't you?"

"No," I told her. "Jordan and I have been too busy making plans."

"I'm so happy for you and Jordan," Lynn said as she did every time I talked to her. "I can understand why you haven't been writing. But you'll have to get cracking on it now and get it finished."

I took a deep breath and let it out, my mind whirling with all the things I had to do in the next few weeks. "Yes, you're right. I will." //

"I'm sure Jordan will understand when you show him the letter. You *have* told him about the book, haven't you?"

"Not yet, Lynn. I really didn't expect this, so I kept putting it off."

"Won't he be surprised?" Her voice sounded warm and happy. "When's he coming back from Virginia?"

"Tomorrow, I hope. He said he'd call if he got delayed."

"Go out to dinner and celebrate," she advised. "Something like this doesn't happen every day."

"You're right," I agreed, smiling. It would be fun to tell Jordan and see his reaction.

"I'm going to hang up and let you get right to work. I'll bring this by on the way home tonight if you want me to. Save you a trip."

"Fine," I told her. "See you then. Stay for supper."

"Nope. I can't interrupt you. You need to get that book finished."

I hung up the phone and went to the kitchen to make a pot of coffee. My surprise had given way to exhilaration. This was going to be a long day and night. Thank goodness I didn't have any typing to do for anyone, even Mr. Hadley.

As I settled myself in my desk chair a few minutes later, that tiny, uneasy feeling assailed me again. *You're just a worrywart,* I told myself, and firmly pushed it down. *There's nothing wrong with anything, so knock it off and get to work.*

At eight o'clock the following evening I opened the front door and Jordan walked in. He smelled of fresh air and sunshine. He wore his usual jeans and T-shirt and looked tanned and fit and wonderful. "I've missed you so much," he said, pulling me to him for a long, tender kiss.

"I've missed you too," I told him. "And I've got something to tell you." I was so tired that I felt like propping up my eyelids with toothpicks. I'd been working on the book with only a few hours off for sleep since the letter from the agent yesterday morning, but I was also excited and eager to tell Jordan all about it.

"I've got something to tell you too," he said, his eyes shining. "Or rather, a proposition to put to you." He gave me another kiss, then moved back a little. "How would you like to live in Virginia for the next few months?"

I forgot my own news in my surprise at what he'd said. "Virginia? What are you talking about?"

He reached for my hands and squeezed them. "I'm talking about the fact that I don't want to spend half my time away from you for several more months. I don't think this project will be finished until after Christmas. Laying pipe under a river is slower work than I expected it to be, and things keep going wrong. We're behind schedule."

I stared at him. "You mean you —"

"I mean I want us to get married right now and move down there until this job is finished. Postpone working on our house and everything else."

I swallowed. "But, Jordan, I have something —"

"You want to teach, I know," he broke in, reaching over and lightly touching my nose. "But the teaching slot won't open up until January, and you don't even know if you'll get it, do you?"

"No, but I'm pretty sure I will, and —" I had to tell him about the book.

"All right," he interrupted again. "I'll concede that to you. If you do get the position and my project isn't finished by then, we'll move back up here. As I told you before, I wouldn't expect you to give up a profession you've worked so hard to educate yourself for."

"Jordan, please listen to me. I said I had some news for you too."

"Sure, but can we go to the kitchen and have some iced tea? I've been craving some of your iced tea for the last two days."

In a minute we were sitting across from each other with our glasses of tea in front of us. Smoke was in Jordan's lap, purring up a storm while Jordan stroked him. He looked across at me, his smile tender and warm. "All right, shoot."

I cleared my throat, not knowing quite how to start, and then decided to plunge right in. "I'm writing a book. I found some old letters of Aunt Edith's, and I've been making a story out of them."

His hand stilled on the cat's back, and he looked at me in surprise. "You're writing a book?"

"Yes. I wrote to half a dozen agents about reading it, and yesterday I got a letter from one who wants to see the book as soon as it's finished." I smiled, inviting him to be as skeptical as I was. "Lynn's saying all kinds of crazy things — maybe it'll be a best-seller and be optioned for a movie. Maybe I'll have to go back to L.A. and write a screenplay," I finished, jokingly.

"Why didn't you tell me about this before?"

I shrugged, a little disappointed at his re-action. "I don't know. I was unsure of myself, I guess. I'd never tried to write a book before."

"But you told Lynn," he said, his voice hardening. "Didn't you think the man you were planning to marry might want to know too?"

"I told Lynn only a few weeks ago," I defended myself, disappointment turning into dismay at the way he was taking this. "Jordan, listen. Let me finish." I took another deep breath. "I want us to postpone getting married for another month or so. Just until I've finished the book."

His face tightened and his eyes narrowed. He put down Smoke and got up from his chair. "Let me get this straight," he said. "You've got some crazy idea that this book of yours is going to be a best-seller, and you'd rather work on it than marry me and be with me."

I shook my head. A knot had formed in my stomach. "No, of course I wouldn't. But since the agent did sound enthusiastic about reading it, I'd be crazy not to go ahead and get it off to her as soon as possible."

His face hardened even more. "So you've been doing this ever since we first met, then. You were writing it when I asked you to work with me on some houses."

I shrugged again. "Yes, but what does that —"

"You said you wanted to teach, that that was so important to you. Why didn't you tell me the truth about this book then? You know how I feel about honesty."

I felt myself getting angry at the way he was reacting. "If you'd let me finish a sentence, I might tell you. I do want to teach. That has nothing to do with this."

"Oh, I think it does, Dana," he said coolly. "It's obvious that this book is more important to you than anything else. Fame and fortune are what you really want. Or is it just the idea of getting back to the bright lights of the city again?"

"You've got it all wrong. You're twisting everything I say."

"Do you know what the odds are against your book ever being published, let alone becoming a best-seller?"

"Of course I do! I just told you that that was Lynn's talk. You and I both know how unlikely that is."

"But even so, you want to postpone our marriage. You don't want to go with me to

Virginia. You want to finish the book."
Each of his words dropped like a stone.

"Yes! I do!" I heard my voice rising, but I couldn't help it. "What on earth is the matter with you, Jordan? I've never seen you act this way before. You're being completely unreasonable."

His eyes bored into mine. "I don't think so. That's what another woman told me a couple of years ago," he said coldly. "When I wouldn't agree to move back to Philly and go to work for her father, she broke our engagement. Her life-style was more important to her than I was. And you seem to be telling me the same thing!"

I stared at him, the anger and resentment leaving me and a deadly coldness replacing them. At last I knew the whole story about Vanessa, and why Jordan had been so wary of me at first. I knew why he'd doubted that I'd stay in Cedar Grove, and why it had taken me so long to convince him I wasn't a city girl at heart.

But it looked as if I never had convinced him of that, after all. We were right back to square one.

"Can't you see that this situation has absolutely nothing to do with that other one?" I asked him, still trying desperately to make some sense out of this. "I'm not asking you to move to a city, or telling you I won't marry you if you don't."

A muscle spasmed in his jaw. "Can you honestly tell me that if, by some chance, your book were successful and you were asked to go back to L.A. and go on a book tour, that you'd turn it down?"

I drew in my breath, then let it out. "That's an extremely remote possibility," I said. "You're being unfair."

"No, I'm not. Just realistic. And you didn't answer me."

I sighed. "No, I can't tell you that, Jordan. Before I decided to study to be a teacher, I wanted to be a writer. I planned to major in journalism in college, but gave it up in favor of being practical. Now, I'm not so sure I did the right thing back then. I've enjoyed working on this book more than anything I've ever done. I won't give it up, and if I'm offered publication, I'd be a fool to turn it down."

"I guess that answers my question." His voice was flat and cold. "You're faced with a choice, just as Vanessa was. And like her, you're choosing the life-style you want over marriage to me. Why didn't you stay out in L.A.?" he asked me bitterly. "Where you belong. Why don't you go back there now?"

I blinked back tears as my fumbling fingers slid the engagement ring off my finger and handed it to him. "Maybe I will," I told him, holding my chin up high. "*You're* the one who's making the choice, Jordan — not me." I tried to keep my voice from trembling, but wasn't successful.

His eyes burned into mine as he took the ring and thrust it into his jeans pocket. He opened his mouth, then closed it again, turned away, and walked out of the room. In a moment I heard the front door close behind him.

Now I knew why I'd had the uneasy feeling that things weren't right. And I also knew why Jordan had never told me he loved me, even when he asked me to marry him.

He didn't love me — not me, Dana Gilbert. No, what he'd loved and wanted was an idealized woman, one who fit his model of a perfect wife. All the pieces fit now, I saw.

I could understand why his experience with Vanessa had left him bitter and wary. My own experience with Bruce had made me cautious too. What I couldn't accept was his determination to fit me into a mold of the wife he wanted.

Smoke rubbed against my ankles as he mewed anxiously. I picked him up and held him under my chin. "I'm lucky I found out how unreasonable Jordan is before we were married," I told him. Now, if I could just convince myself of that fact. Maybe I wasn't cut out for small-town living, as Jordan had always thought. I knew that in a few days everyone in town would know about our broken engagement. They'd gossip and speculate about it endlessly. In L.A. no one would know or care. And how could I stay here, knowing I'd see Jordan around town, at the band concerts, at the grocery store? Because I still loved him — even if he had never really loved me.

Chapter Ten

"Can you believe that man really expects me to give up the house I've lived in for forty years and move into his tiny apartment?"

Blythe was so indignant that she stabbed her fork into the slice she'd cut from the lemon pie she'd brought over to me. The pie was piled high with fluffy white meringue, and I knew it would be delicious, but I had little appetite these days.

"I'm sure it would be a very hard thing for you to do," I told her.

"Hard? It would be crazy! Why in the world should we do that? My house is paid for and we've got plenty of room to spread out in. I'd never get all my belongings in an apartment and I don't want to get rid of anything."

I tried to forget my own problems and help with hers. Thomas's expectations might be unreasonable, but it was, after all, just one complaint, which they could probably resolve. *My* problems with Jordan went deeper than that; they went to the very core of his feelings for me.

"Why does Thomas want you to sell the house?" I asked her, hoping she wouldn't pick up on my depression.

"He says a big house ties you down too much. He wants to be able to take off on a trip whenever he feels like it. Says he wants to see the whole country before he dies."

"Don't you like to travel at all? Maybe you'd enjoy it too," I suggested.

She shrugged. "I wouldn't mind a trip once in a while, but I don't like staying in motels and eating out at restaurants. I enjoy cooking and baking and tending my garden and flowers. Thomas knows all this. That was one of the first things that drew us together. He loves to grow things too. That's why I can't understand him acting this way."

"What if you sold your house and bought a smaller one — with room for a garden and flowers but not so much trouble to take care of?" I suggested.

Blythe immediately shook her head again. "No, that just wouldn't do. It wouldn't be the same." She gave me a sheepish look. "Do you think I'm being as unreasonable as Thomas?" she asked.

I smiled at her. "No, I just think that if you two care about each other enough to get married, you can solve this problem. After all, he's not asking you to move away from Cedar Grove."

She cocked her head, thought for a moment, then glanced up at me. "You know, you've got a good point there. I think I'll go home and call Thomas and ask him to come over to talk about this."

"Good. I bet you'll be able to work something out."

Now that her own worries were possibly on the way to being settled, she looked at me more closely. "What's wrong, Dana? You look a little peaked around the gills."

I tried to laugh at her no doubt quite apt description of my appearance. "I guess I am." I held out my ringless left hand. "Jordan and I broke up last week."

"That's awful! What in the world happened? Maybe I can give you some good advice too."

I hesitated, really not wanting to mention my book and all the other stuff, but finally decided I shouldn't have said as much as I had if I didn't want to tell her everything.

"Well, that does beat all," she said when I'd finished. "All those years I knew Edith, and she never breathed a word about anything like that. And you're writing a book about it?" She shook her head, then patted my arm. "Let's get back to the important thing — the way Jordan acted when you told him about it. Sounds like the boy had a real bad experience with that other woman, doesn't it?"

I sighed and nodded. "I'm sure he did, but that has nothing to do with us. He can't see that I'm not the same kind of person, that this isn't at all like *that* situation."

And it looked as if he never would. For three mornings after we'd broken up, I saw Jordan exercising the horses in the fields. On the fourth morning he phoned, his voice stiff and cool, and told me he was off to Virginia for a few days. He asked me if I wanted him to hire someone to tend the horses, and I told him that of course I'd do it. He thanked me and hung up, and that ended that.

Blythe sighed and shook her head. "Now that I've heard your problems, mine don't seem nearly as bad. I wish I could tell you something that would make you feel better, but I can't think of a thing except that maybe Jordan will realize how wrong he is if you give him some time."

I didn't think so. Jordan struck me as a very stubborn man. When his mind was made up, no matter how wrong he was, it stayed made up. "Maybe so, Blythe," I answered, forcing a smile as I walked her to the door.

I cleaned up our dishes, then made more

coffee. After Jordan left that awful day, I was so miserable that I wondered how I'd ever finish the book. It no longer seemed important, even though that was what we'd broken up over.

But I knew that the book wasn't the real reason. And I was going to be professional about this. I'd asked the agent to read it, and she'd agreed, and so I would finish it if it killed me.

Smoke woke up from a nap on his favorite spot this week, the rug in front of the sink, and gave me one of his greeting sounds. He looked at me a moment as if wondering if it was too much trouble to get up and demand some food. Then he yawned and closed his eyes again, apparently deciding it was.

I thought of Jordan and, instead of depression, I felt anger now. I'd been alternating between those two emotions all week. "Pigheaded darn man!" I muttered, pouring myself a large mug of coffee. "I'm going to the band concert on Saturday too," I told the sink. "You're not going to spoil everything in life for me."

I took the coffee to my office and settled down before the desk. I *would* finish this blasted book. And I'd do a good job of it too. Maybe it would never sell, but at least I'd have the satisfaction of knowing I'd done my very best to realize the dream in my mind.

Six days later I walked into the post office with a large padded envelope. "There you are," I told Lynn, plunking it down on the window ledge. "It's all ready to go."

Out of the corner of my eye I saw an elderly woman who was manipulating the dials on her mailbox. She paused to give us an interested look.

Lynn's face lit up in a wide smile. "That's great. I'll weigh it for you and send it priority mail. That way it will take only two days to get to New York."

"I need return postage too."

"Okay, but she's not going to return the book. She's going to love it and send it out to an editor, and it's going to sell just like that." Lynn snapped her fingers briskly, then put the envelope on the scales.

The elderly woman had stopped working the dials on her box and was favoring us with her undivided attention. Lynn looked over my shoulder and smiled at her. "Can I help you, Mrs. Hamilton?" she asked.

"Uh, no, no, I was just going," Mrs. Hamilton said. Her eyes were bright, and, smiling at both of us, she hurried out.

Lynn glanced at her box and shook her

head. "She was so excited she forgot to take her mail. I guess you know what this means?"

"Yes. By tomorrow morning it'll be all over town that I've written a book and sent it off to New York."

Lynn grinned. "You underestimate the efficiency of the Cedar Grove grapevine. By tomorrow morning it will be all over town that you've *sold* a book, and by tomorrow night it will be a bestseller."

Her grin faded and she gave me a serious look. "All kidding aside, Dana, I really do think this will sell. It's darned good."

"You haven't read the ending," I told her darkly. "I never could get it just the way I wanted it."

"I bet it's fine. You just have no confidence in your ability."

I heard the door open behind me. Lynn glanced over, then her face tightened. I didn't have to turn around to know that Jordan had just walked in. I felt myself tense from the top of my head to my feet.

"Hello, Jordan," Lynn said, icicles dripping from her voice.

"Hello, Lynn . . . Dana." His voice sounded strained.

I forced myself to paste a smile on my face and turn around. "Hi, Jordan."

He had dark circles under his eyes, and

his face looked tired and tense. I felt my heart begin to melt a little. Why were we doing this to each other? I cleared my throat and asked, "How've you been?"

He shrugged, his face expressionless. "All right." He kept on looking at me, and then I thought his face changed a little, as if he were going to say something else. But he didn't. Instead, he turned away and started twirling the dials on his mailbox.

"I've got to go," I told Lynn, swallowing the lump in my throat. I headed for the door, not looking at Jordan.

"Wait a minute, Dana," Jordan said as I turned the knob. "I want to talk to you."

I felt my heart leap with hope as I glanced back at him. Was Blythe right, then? Had Jordan just needed some time to think things over? I nodded. "All right," I answered, carefully keeping my voice casual.

"I have to go back to Virginia today," he said. "I'll be gone for a week. When I get back, we need to get together so I can pay you for pasturing the horses."

"You need to pay me?" I echoed stupidly, feeling like a fool for what I'd just thought he was going to say.

"Yes. I'm taking them out to my land in the valley."

"You don't owe me, Jordan," I said

crisply. "I owe you, if anything. I've never paid you for the materials you used in repairing my house." I lifted my chin and met his gaze squarely.

"Don't worry about that. Shall we call it even, then?"

"Fine with me."

Behind me, Lynn rattled paper loudly. "Your book will go out in the morning's mail, Dana," she said. "Since you're sending it priority mail, it should get to New York in two days."

I knew she was repeating this for Jordan's benefit, letting him know that I hadn't been crushed by our breakup, that I was going ahead with my life.

All I wanted to do was escape from here and go home. Feeling tears behind my eyelids, I said, "Thanks, Lynn." I opened the door and went out, wishing I'd never left California.

And with all my heart, I wished I'd never met Jordan Meade.

"I just can't stand the thought of your leaving Cedar Grove," Blythe said, looking around my disheveled kitchen. She carried a napkin-covered plate and set it on the table after moving a stack of dishes aside to find room. "I brought you some cinnamon rolls."

181

I gave her a tired smile, then pushed back the hair straggling down on my neck. "Thanks, Blythe, that's great. I won't have to worry about breakfast."

She ran a critical eye down me. "You don't look like you've been eating anything. You must have lost ten pounds."

I shrugged. "You know what they say — you can never be too thin or too rich. Since I don't have much hope of ever being rich, I guess I'll have to settle for the other."

She shook her head. "I still don't see why you're moving to Philadelphia."

"It's best," I told her. "I'll come back to visit often." I was afraid it was an idle promise. I doubted if I'd do that.

"Did you find a teaching job?" she asked, sitting down on a kitchen chair.

I nodded and sat down too. I'd been packing since early morning and was exhausted. "Yes, I was very lucky. A teacher at one of the elementary schools is leaving and I was able to get the position. Second grade — just the one I wanted too."

"What about your book? Have you heard anything yet?"

"No, but it's been only two weeks. I didn't expect to this soon."

She smiled and patted my shoulder. "I bet you will sell it, though."

"I won't hold my breath waiting," I told her with a wry smile.

"I hate to sound so happy when things didn't work out for you and Jordan, but I wanted to tell you that Thomas and I are getting married next week."

"That's wonderful, Blythe! So I guess you settled the house problem."

"Yes, we did."

"What did you decide on — a smaller house?"

"Nope. We're going to buy a motor home. Thomas agreed to live in my house, so I agreed to go on several trips with him during the year." She added in amazement, "Those motor homes have just everything you could want — kitchens and baths and all. It's like a little apartment."

"Yes, I guess that's true. I'm sure you're going to be very happy, Blythe."

"I think so too. I just wish you and Jordan. . . ."

"Don't worry about me," I told her briskly. "Some things just aren't meant to be, I guess. I'll do fine."

She sighed, patted my knee, and got up. "I know you will. Well, you be sure and come say good-bye before you leave."

"Of course I will." I walked with her to the door, evading the cartons piled everywhere. Smoke poked his head up from the top of one and greeted me. He'd been in seventh heaven with all the boxes around for him to investigate and sleep in.

I took a deep breath and headed back to the kitchen, where I still had more to pack. I hoped Lynn didn't call again this evening and try to change my mind about moving. She still couldn't believe I meant it.

But that last scene at the post office with Jordan had made me realize that I couldn't bear to spend the rest of my life living in the same town with him. There was no way we could avoid each other. Cedar Grove was too small.

Nor could I bear to go to the band concerts on Saturday nights and listen to him play his saxophone. I'd realized that last Saturday night, when I'd gone with Lynn. Jordan hadn't been there — still in Virginia, I supposed — and I'd been much relieved. This had made me realize that the only way I could get on with my life was to get away from here.

Of course the expense of moving back to L.A. was out of the question, but if I could rent this house and find a job in Philadelphia, I could swing it. As I'd told Blythe, I'd been very lucky. A few telephone inquiries and a day's trip to the city had landed me a job and an apartment I could afford. I didn't have the house rented yet, but school would soon start and I'd have my salary from that.

So, I was getting on with my life. And it would be a long time, indeed, before I got involved with another man. Once burned was bad enough, but *twice?* I folded back the flaps of yet another carton and lifted in a stack of pots and pans, trying to summon some enthusiasm.

When a knock sounded on the door, I sighed and glanced at my watch. Six. It was no doubt Lynn, stopping by after work to try to wear me down some more.

I trudged to the door and pulled it open, steeling myself to tell Lynn she was welcome to come in if she'd leave me alone.

Jordan stood there in his jeans and a white T-shirt. His hair looked longer than I remembered it, as if he hadn't bothered with getting it cut. He still had the dark circles under his eyes. And he still made my heart turn over just to look at him. Why was he here?

"May I come in?" he asked finally.

I realized I'd been staring, and stepped back a little, bumping into a carton. I was suddenly conscious of my rumpled green shirt, my straggly hair, my no doubt smudged face. "Of course."

I knew why he was here — to talk about the horses. Trying to ignore the way my heart had plummeted, I led the way into the cluttered dining room. Then I saw that Jordan wasn't following me.

I turned to see him staring at the half-filled cartons and the piles of objects on every available surface. "What's all this?" he asked. "Are you moving away?"

I'd thought he already knew. "Yes," I said.

Smoke reached out a lazy paw from a nearby carton and swiped affectionately at Jordan's bare arm. Jordan ran his hand down the cat's back. For some reason, that small gesture almost undid me. I swallowed a huge lump in my throat and, pretending I hadn't seen it, continued to the kitchen.

"Well," I said briskly, turning to face him as we reached a relatively clear space of kitchen floor, "I suppose you want to talk about the horses. You can leave them here until I move next week. Probably longer. I don't have the house rented yet."

He didn't answer. He looked around the kitchen, which was in more disarray than the dining room. Finally he turned back to me. "Why are you doing this, Dana?" He moved a step closer to me, his face tightening. "I thought you were planning to

186

make Cedar Grove your home. You certainly said so often enough."

I stared at him, a wave of exhaustion sweeping over me. I sat down on one of the kitchen chairs before I fell down. "I wouldn't think you'd have to ask that question," I finally answered, relieved that my voice sounded cool and concealed my inner turmoil.

"So you've sold the book and are headed back to L.A. You're wiping the dust of Cedar Grove from your feet."

I was so miserable and unhappy that I wanted to throw something at him. But I was also too tired to get up and find anything. I settled for glaring at him. "No, I didn't sell the book. And I'm not moving back to L.A. Because I can't afford to. I'm moving to Philadelphia."

"Philadelphia?" he asked, sounding surprised. "Why?"

Was he deliberately trying to torture me? I got up and stood in front of him, my hands on my hips. "You know very well why, Jordan. Because I can't stand to live in the same town you're in!"

"So you hate me that much, do you?" he asked. His voice was cold now. As cold as ice.

I knew I wasn't going to be able to hold

back the tears much longer. "You are the most obtuse, stubborn man I've ever seen," I told him, my voice trembling. "You never did love me, did you? You never even *knew* me. Now, will you get out of here? I still have a lot of packing to do."

He stood there staring at me for a moment longer. Then he turned and threaded his way through the maze of boxes and disappeared into the dining room. In a few moments I heard the front door open and close.

I blinked and the tears behind my eyelids rolled down my cheeks. I let them fall, too dejected to care. If I'd ever had any doubts about everything being over between us, I no longer did.

Smoke jumped down from his carton and rubbed against my ankles, making anxious little sounds of distress. I picked him up and cuddled him, looking around the chaotic room.

Then the phone rang. I knew it had to be Lynn with another last-ditch try at persuading me to stay here. I just couldn't take any more today.

"Hold the fort," I told Smoke, putting him on the floor. "I'll be back in a little while." I jerked the back door open and slammed it behind me, then hurried through the yard to the field. Sally was way down in the lower field, but Ranger was nearby.

"Come on," I told him, and he followed me to the barn. I grabbed a bridle from a hook and quickly fastened the straps. Then I threw a saddle pad across his broad back. I started to lift the heavy Western saddle, then stopped. I'd never ridden Ranger with just a pad, but I had Sally, several times.

It would be all right, I told myself as I led him out of the barn and then climbed onto his back. Ranger was used to me now. I urged him into a canter and then a gallop. Soon we were racing down the slope to the lower field. It was getting late and the sky was almost dark. A breeze had come up and it felt good. As it blew my hair back from my hot face, I leaned over Ranger's neck, urging him on.

Sally looked up, whinnied, and came running to meet us. Then a piece of paper came floating through the air, straight for Ranger's head. I sucked in my breath, remembering Jordan's warning that Ranger would shy at this kind of thing. He neighed, and then before I knew what was happening, he reared.

I felt myself slipping sideways, and I clutched at his flanks with my knees. But it was no use. I had just enough time to let go of the reins so that I wouldn't get tangled in them. And then the ground came up to meet me. Ranger headed for the barn, with Sally galloping beside him.

I'd landed on my side with my left leg doubled up under me. I lay there for a few minutes, winded, and with a sharp pain throbbing through my leg and foot. Finally, I eased myself up to a sitting position, which made everything hurt even worse.

Well, Dana, you've done it this time, I thought, carefully stretching my leg out in front of me. That brought on the pain again, but I felt a little of my fear ebb. I didn't think my leg was broken. I eased my sneaker and sock off. My ankle and foot were already swelling and beginning to turn purple.

I tried to decide what to do. If I'd broken something, then walking back to the house would probably cause further damage. I wasn't even sure I could do it.

If that *had* been Lynn on the phone, then she might come out to the house. But I couldn't be sure of that, or that I could make enough noise for her to find me all the way down here. I wasn't even sure it had been she. I could sit here all night and no one would find me. It was dark now, and I didn't much like that idea, even though an almost-full moon was rising.

I might as well face it: I had to get myself out of this mess. I moved my leg again, experimentally, and winced as a fresh wave of pain made sweat break out on my forehead.

How was I going to do it? Should I try to crawl, dragging my hurt leg and foot? That thought made me shudder, because just moving my leg hurt so much. Could I hop on my good leg? It was worth a try, I decided.

I eased myself over onto my stomach, then pushed myself up onto my right leg and tried to balance. My arms flailed wildly and my injured foot connected with the ground with a bone-jarring jolt. I quickly sat down again as tears of pain filled my eyes.

That wasn't a very bright thing to do, I scolded myself. Closing my eyes, I waited for the pain to subside.

"What do you think you're doing?" Jordan growled from close by.

My eyes flew open to find him crouched in front of me. I gulped and asked, "What are you doing here?"

"Looking for you, of course," he said curtly. "Let's see what you've done to that foot." He reached for my foot and carefully began to feel it.

"How did you know I was down here?" I asked.

"You didn't answer the door when I knocked, but all the lights were on, so I went inside. When I couldn't find you, I walked out back, just in time to see Ranger tearing up toward the barn with nothing but a bridle on. I aged ten years in five minutes." He glared at me, then took his hands off my foot and sat down in front of me, his legs crossed.

"Why were you looking for me?" I asked him.

He looked at me for a long time, as if trying to make up his mind what to say. "Walking home, it occurred to me that I might have misinterpreted what you said about why you were leaving," he said finally. "Why do you think I was taking the horses to my house in the valley?"

"I don't know."

"Because I planned to move into the house, just to get away from Cedar Grove where *you* were."

Coldness invaded my bones. "Oh," I said. "I see."

He shook his head. "No, I don't think you do. I knew I couldn't bear to see you around town, Dana, because I love you and it would tear my heart out to see you and not be with

192

you." He reached out a gentle hand and touched my cheek.

I took a deep breath and let it out. "What did you just say? I think I misunderstood you."

"No, you didn't. Did you think I could stop loving you just like that?"

A warm, wonderful feeling was spreading through me. I forgot about my foot. "I didn't think you loved me at all. Not the *real* me, anyway."

His hand reached for one of mine, then he covered it with his other hand. "I've been a stupid, arrogant fool," he told me. "Will you let me try to explain why?"

I smiled at him. "All right," I said, moving my foot a little. I bit my lip as the movement brought on another throbbing pain.

Jordan released my hand and got up. "But not until we get you to the house. I'm not sure if your foot is broken or just sprained. I'm going to carry you."

I started to object, then decided he was right.

He lifted me, slowly and carefully, and I put my arms around his neck and held on tight as he walked to the house. I felt his heart beating beneath my cheek, and was comforted by his warm, strong arms as they held me close.

Once at the house, Jordan threaded his way between the cartons and into the living room, where he carefully deposited me on the couch. "Do you have an ice bag and some elastic bandages?" he asked.

I told him where to find them, and in a few minutes my foot and ankle were wrapped, with the ice bag on top.

Then he sat down at the other end of the couch. "I told you about Vanessa, and you saw firsthand how my father still won't accept my decision to leave the family business and move away from Philly." I nodded and he continued. "I got completely fed up with anything big-city after those two battles. I settled down in Cedar Grove, determined that if I ever got serious about a woman again, it would be someone who could share small-town life with me, who'd be happy and content living here."

I nodded again, and said nothing.

"Then you moved here, with your big-city background, your sophistication, and all the things I swore I'd never have any dealings with again."

I blinked in disbelief. "You think I'm sophisticated?" I asked. "Me?"

He smiled and reached for my hand. "All right, I was off-base on that. But I still couldn't quite believe you'd stay here permanently. I was afraid you'd get tired of sleepy little Cedar Grove and head back to the bright lights." He paused and gave me a wry smile. "That's why I acted like such a jackass when you told me about your book and the stuff Lynn was saying about movie deals. The only thing I could see was your leaving me, going back to L.A., and demanding I go along or forget the marriage."

My stomach began to tense. So here we were back to the real problem. I gave him a straight look. "I'd never do that, Jordan. I don't want to leave here, either." Then I took a deep breath and let it out. "But you know I sent my book off. I don't know what's going to happen with it. But I do know one thing — I'm going to continue writing."

He squeezed my hand. "I can accept that now. That day at the post office, I realized how much I'd missed you and loved you. But I still couldn't quite make my stubborn self admit I was wrong." He gave me a wry smile. "The last few days in Virginia, I did a lot of thinking. And I finally realized that I'd acted with you just like my father did with me. I was demanding you give up something you wanted and needed to do." He paused, and then his eyes looked straight into mine. "I want to marry you, whatever compromises we have to work out."

The knot in my stomach was dissolving, but there were still a few things I didn't understand. "Why didn't you tell me that earlier tonight?" I asked.

"I planned to. But when I walked in and saw you were all packed up to move, it threw me. Then you told me you were leaving because you couldn't stand to be in the same town with me, and I was sure I'd waited too long, that you'd stopped loving me."

"I tried to. Believe me, I tried. But it just didn't work. That's why I was leaving."

"As I told you down in the field, that thought occurred to me as I was walking home." He stopped talking and we just looked at each other.

Then Jordan moved up beside me and took me into his arms and kissed me long and deeply. When he finally drew away, I was breathless. But happier than I'd ever been in my life.

"I think I'd better take you to the emergency room to have your foot checked," he said huskily.

My foot turned out to be broken, after all. Jordan sat with me at the hospital and held my hand while my foot was examined and put into a cast. Then he took me home and slept on the sofa all night in case I needed anything.

In the morning he brought me breakfast in bed. "You're going to spoil me," I told him as he put the tray on my lap, and gave me a good-morning kiss.

"That's all right," he said, and kissed me again. Then as he dug in his pocket, a frown drew his brows together. He tried his other pockets, and finally pulled out my ring. Relief washed over his face. "I've carried your ring in my pocket ever since we split up," he said. "I was afraid for a moment that I'd lost it."

I grinned at him as he slipped it back on my finger. "I'm glad you didn't," I said, "because I love this ring. But if you had lost it, it wouldn't have been a tragedy. It's the promise that matters."

My smile faded as our eyes met in a long, tender look.

"I love you, Dana," he said, leaning toward me.

"And I love you, Jordan," I answered.

"If you have to go anywhere, I'll go with you," he said. "Wherever you are will be home to me."

I tipped my head up to meet him halfway. Our hearts had found a home in each other. And that was all that mattered.